MW01600639

# Valentine's Day With My Landlord

CHARISSE C. CARR

# *Introduction*

Dear Readers...

This is a rerelease. Valentine's Day With My Landlord was my second book when I became a published author. If you are reading this again, thank you for your continued support. If this is your first time, welcome and prepare to laugh as Delilah takes you on a hilarious, literary ride.

**Copyright © 2024 by Charisse C. Carr**

**All rights reserved.**

Any unauthorized reprint or use of the material is prohibited. No part of this book may be reproduced or transmitted in any form or by any means, electronic or mechanical, including photocopying, recording, or by any information storage and retrieval systems, without written permission by the author, except for the use of brief quotations in a book review.

This is an original work of fiction. Names, characters, places, and incidents are either products of the author's imagination or are used fictitiously, and any resemblance to actual persons, living or dead, is entirely coincidental.

*Chapter One*

DELILAH JONES

"Y ou betta get up and get yo ass over here! The repo man outside tryna take your car!" My mom was screaming at the top of her lungs.

"Don't let them take it, momma. I just need to throw my clothes on, and I'm out the door."

It was too early in the morning for the bullshit. I didn't even wipe the crust out of my eyes yet, and now I had to deal with this mess.

Jumping out of my bed, I threw on whatever I could find. I didn't have time to brush my teeth or my hair. If I didn't get my ass over to my mom's house, they were going to take my damn car, and that was the last thing I needed.

I fell behind on my payments, and the *Buy Here, Pay Here* people were on my ass. You couldn't miss one month with them. That was what I owed, well, two months now. These muthafuckas tried to take my car two weeks ago from right outside my house.

My sons came banging on the door while I was in the shower. They were yelling that someone was trying to steal my car. I knew exactly who it was and didn't have time to dry off or get dressed.

I ran to the linen closet, grabbed a sheet, and wrapped myself up like a burrito. There wasn't enough time to put my shoes on, so I had to Fred Flintstone it. I snatched my keys and ran outside. My sons followed right behind me.

The repo man didn't have my car hooked up yet, so I hollered to my sons to get in the car. I started that bitch up and drove the fuck off. He was mad as hell. I flipped him the bird as I rode by. We circled the block a few times until the repo man finally left.

Now, here I go again! This time I was going to have to make a run for it, literally. My momma only lived two blocks over. I was five feet six inches, weighing in at 230 pounds. It was going to be more of a jog than actual running. I used to be in better shape before I lost my job three months ago. During that time I picked up thirty pounds, drowning my sorrows in food.

The kids were still sleeping. I should be back before they wake up. Racing down my front steps and out of the gate, I took off like I was being chased by wild, rabid dogs. If they really were after me, my ass would have been caught. I only made it to the end of my block before I had to stop. I started wheezing like I was about to have an asthma attack, but I didn't even have asthma. I took two deep breaths, then was off again.

"Where are you running off to? You better slow down before your big ass passes out!"

"Go to hell, Mrs. Johnson." I was doing a slow jog now, so I knew she heard me. I couldn't stand her old ass. She always had something smart to say. All she did was sit on her porch all day long fucking with people as they passed by.

I was almost at my mom's house and could see the repo man hooking up my car. She was outside going the fuck off on him. Her loud ass screamed and threatened to call the cops, but he wasn't paying her any mind at all. If unbothered was a person, it would be him.

"Sir, kind sir. Please don't take my car. I'm 'bout to pay what I owe next week." I yelled, panting and lying, as I bent over and rested my hands on my knees. I wasn't paying shit next week. I couldn't even afford to pay attention.

"Ma'am, I have orders to take this car. I know it's almost Valentine's Day, and I do have a heart. I just don't take kindly to disrespect." Once he said that, I realized he was the same mutha-fucka that showed up to my house two weeks ago.

"Listen, I apologize for giving you the finger. I was in the middle of scrubbing my ass when you showed up and meant no harm." I gave him the saddest looking face I could muster up. Hopefully, he'd take pity on my miserable ass.

"I get it, no one wants their car taken away. I accept your

apology, and I know you were just acting off of raw emotions." I started smiling hard as hell.

"Now, with that being said, I need you to back the fuck on up!" he barked, raising his left eyebrow as he lifted my car onto the back of the tow truck.

I just stood there looking unkempt while he climbed back into his tow truck and drove away with my car. The bastard was laughing too. He also had the nerve to flip me the bird. I picked up a skateboard that was laying on the sidewalk and threw it. That sucka barely went two feet in the air. I had no fight left in me.

Fuck! I didn't think they would find my car at my momma's house. I used her as a co-signer, so they must have figured to come over here too. Now,I had no way to get me and my kids around. I felt like such a failure. It was just one thing after the other.

"You look like shit. Here, take this water and drink it. I know your throat is probably dry as hell." My momma was so blunt and didn't mind hurting my feelings. But I did appreciate her calling me and trying to help.

"Thank you! You were out here acting a straight fool. I know he wanted to run your ass over." I giggled as I took a sip of water.

"He's lucky I didn't pull out my taser. I woulda put that bitch on the side of his neck and sent electric currents down to his ass cheeks. I don't wanna sit in nobody's jail, so I didn't." My momma was crazy as hell. She was known for stunning the shit out of you.

She was banned from playing bingo at our local church for pulling it out on Mr. Cox. My mom threatened to shock his balls when she was the one who was wrong. Her ass thought she had bingo and didn't. He came over to check her card, and said she stamped the wrong number. She lost her mind and had to be escorted out. I was so embarrassed because I was sitting right next to her when this happened and had to leave too because I was her ride home.

"Well, I'm gonna head on back. I left the kids in the house by themselves."

"You wanna come inside first and fix yourself up? Your hair looks like giraffes have been licking on it. And what the hell do you have on? Nothing matches."

My getup did scream homeless. I had on a pair of rainbow striped leggings that showed every nook and cranny, a black T-shirt with holes in it, gold rain boots, and a charcoal gray pea coat I should have thrown away two winters ago.

I followed my mom into her house. She had a two bedroom, even though it was just her. Well, she let my sister move in with her two kids. That was a whole other story. I just needed to fix my hair and get the hell up out of here.

When I went into the bathroom to do my hair, I opened the cabinet under the sink and shit was everywhere. One of my nieces did this, or it might have been both of them. Edge control containers were open and stuff was dumped out all over the place. They had put hair grease all over every damn thing.

The tub was full of naked Barbie dolls with their hair slicked down. My sister just let her kids do whatever. Her dirty ass didn't even clean the tub out. We were all supposed to get together for dinner here tomorrow, but I didn't even want to come back after seeing this shit. I wasn't in a celebratory mood anyway, especially after they took my car.

"Momma, do you have a hat for me? I was gonna do my hair, but Denise's kids had a field day in your bathroom. You're gonna be mad as hell when you go in there." I chuckled, but wasn't shit funny.

"Dee, I know." That's the nickname I had that everyone called me, but my name was Delilah. Delilah Jones. "I already went in there when I got up to use the bathroom. That's how I heard the repo man outside. One of them opened up my damn window in the dead of winter, letting all my heat out!"

You could hear the frustration in my momma's voice.

"Denise was probably smoking a cigarette. You know she had that habit for years. Always smelling like old ashtrays and chimney smoke." I frowned my face up just thinking about it.

She was one of those smokers that lit up on their way to your car, took a few pulls, and then would get right in the car, reeking of the carcinogens. And don't let her be drinking coffee too. That was the worst combo in the world. When she talked, it was like people made out of shit were breathing on you. That funky ass breath would melt your eyebrows right off your face.

"You're probably right, and I'll tell you what. If I catch her smokin' in my muthafuckin' house, I'm gonna punch her right in her shit!" My momma bawled up her fist and held it up as she spoke.

She was lying, though, and wasn't gonna do shit to Denise.

Now, if that was me, she would have. My mom was quick with her hands and didn't care how old I was.

I remembered that time I was yelling at my kids because they weren't listening. My mom told me to hush up all that noise in her house and to leave them alone. I told her those were my kids, and I will discipline them how I damn well please. They never got hit. I just got loud and made a lot of empty threats.

Before I could finish my sentence, she came across the room and busted me upside my head. My mom hit me so hard, I bit down on my tongue. I wanted to power drive her ass into the ground.

"Well, can you give me a hat, so I can be on my way? The kids are probably up by now, looking for me. I don't even have my cell phone on me."

"There's one hanging up by the door. Grab it on your way out. You can bring it back tomorrow."

Kissing my mom goodbye, I headed back home. As I was walking, I started thinking about how I even got into this predicament in the first place. I used to work at Big Worm's Rump Shakers as a plus size dancer.

I was his bottom bitch, racking and stacking. Every Thursday, Friday, and Saturday night I hit that stage. *Tambourine* by Eve was my opening song every time. When that beat dropped, so did my ass. Now, the only tambourine I shook was in the church choir on Sundays.

*It was a Saturday night, so the place was packed. One of our V.I.P.s was having his birthday bash at our establishment. This* was a big deal for us because it meant a huge pay day. He requested the two top dancers. Of course that would be myself and Keema's dog face ass. She might look like she ate puppy chow, but Keema could dance her ass off. She definitely understood the assignment and showed out every time she hit the stage.

Well, Keema and I were in the back getting changed. It was ten minutes before showtime. I had this bad ass three piece set made specifically for this night. It consisted of a bra, thong, and boy shorts and was bedazzled in Caribbean blue opal and Indian pink Swarovski crystals. I was about to shine brighter than the North Star. Keema knew it, and so did her rat face ass sister, Kayla.

They both were eyeing me as I sprayed body glitter all over myself. Kayla only worked here because she was Keema's sister. She couldn't dance worth a damn. It looked like she was having a seizure when she shook her lil rump. I was surprised she showed up tonight. Normally, she was off on weekends. Big Worm only had her working the slow days, with her discombobulated ass.

Only time she made a decent bag was when she did private dances in the champagne room. We all knew she was in there letting them suck farts out of her ass. She definitely cashed in during those times. It was a good thing too because she would never work the V.I.P. area, not on my watch.

Now, when you danced for any V.I.P, you knew you were about to cash in as well. Everyone in that section came to make it rain on your ass; a straight downpour. Plus, Big Worm gave each dancer a bonus. You received ten percent of the profit made off the bar during your set. That was a nice lil chunk of change. They never spared any expense when it came to bottle service.

Private dances were requested during this time too. Ten times outta ten, they wanted me. I wasn't fucking, and I damn sure wasn't sucking, but I always got the job done. Even though I didn't use my mouth, I earned the nickname Jaws of Life because I was in there extracting souls. My hand skills were A-1. I had a purple bag that I prepped before every V.I.P. performance. It contained everything I needed to make that man have an outer body experience.

I'd have him lay back on the oversized couch and spread his wings like an eagle. I wiped his dick down with a warm cloth I kept in an insulated bag. After it was nice and clean, and standing at attention, I put a condom on it. No one would get the chance to scatter their seeds all over my face like it was a garden.

I took out my homemade coconut and lavender body oil and put some in my hand, rubbing a thin layer of it on both of his inner thighs. While giving him a nice, long massage, I slowly grazed my fingers up and down his legs and stared into his eyes. This drove him crazy! I hadn't come across one man yet that didn't enjoy that part.

The sexual tension building made him want to jump out of his skin. He would beg for me to stroke him, but making him wait added to the excitement of what was to come.

I grabbed an ice cube from the insulated cup I kept them in and placed it on the little erogenous area between his ass and balls. If you wanted to be technical, it was called the perineum. But weren't being technical, just nasty.

*Rubbing this area sent chills up his spine, and his dick became harder than a steel rod. At this time, I took a hold of his shaft with my right hand while replacing the ice cube with my left pointer finger. While slowly applying gentle forward strokes to this sensitive area, I stroked his manhood with a firm grip.*

*The massage oil that was still on my hand allowed it to glide up and down with ease. He was ready to bust at this point, so I increased my strokes and the pressure I applied to that little patch of pleasure.*

*He would explode like a rocket ship into space; rolling over into the fetal position as his body spasmed uncontrollably. I took out another warm cloth, cleaned him up, and collected my cash. They always put a lil cherry on top.*

*Those two hoes saw me grab my purple bag, so they knew I was going for broke. There was no sharing of the funds from the champagne room, and I planned on cashing in tonight.*

*"Bitch, are you ready to go light this shit up?" Keema questioned as she walked behind me.*

*"You know I stay ready. It's demon time. Let's go get 'em!"*

*As I was walking, I felt some sort of mist hit my ass cheeks that were peeking out from my boy shorts. I looked back over my shoulder and saw Keema spraying me with something.*

*"What the fuck are you doing, hoe?" I questioned, looking back at her.*

*"It's just a lil perfume. When you throw that ass in a circle, you will smell like wild flowers. I sprayed myself too." She had a sinister grin on her face. I didn't have time to play any games*

*with her sneaky ass, so I just kept on walking. It was showtime, and we couldn't keep them waiting!*

*We made it to the V.I.P. section, and it was packed. All I saw were dollar signs. I sat my bag down and headed straight to the man of the hour. I signaled to the DJ to drop that beat, and it was on. I turned around, putting my ass in his face. Next thing I knew, he pushed me straight to the ground.*

*"What the fuck is that odor? Baby girl, you out here smelling like wild animal kingdom."*

*"Nigga is you crazy! I know it's ya birthday but if you ever put your hands on me again, I will gut yo ass like a fish." I picked myself up from off the floor.*

*"I apologize for my reaction, but yo ass stink. That smell is stronger than cat piss. It's like you gotta wolf pussy or some shit."*

*I reached my hand back, swiping it across my ass where Keema sprayed me at. I put my fingers toward my nose and almost passed out. No wonder he pushed me out of his face. That rancid ass smell was lethal. Keema did this shit on purpose! I looked over at her, and she was laughing so hard she snorted.*

*I lunged at her but was pulled back by my bra strap. When I turned my head around, like the exorcist, to see who had hemmed me up, it was Big Worm's grimy ass! I stomped on his foot with my damn heel, putting all my weight on it. Then I elbowed him in one of his titties. They were bigger than mine. He yelled out in pain, letting me go.*

*Keema tried to get away, but I was on her ass. I snatched that bitch by those raggedy ass braids she had in her hair, two months too long, with both my hands. We fell into the DJ booth, but that didn't stop me, though. I rolled on top of her, straddled her like a cowgirl about to rope cattle, and repeatedly punched her in her chest.*

*Before I could choke her out, security pulled me off her. They escorted me back to the locker room. Big Worm was behind them screaming for me to get my shit and get out of his place of business. He threw my purple bag at me. Security stood outside the locker room door while I changed back into my clothes.*

*I was getting ready to leave when I noticed that Keema's locker was unlocked. I opened it up and inside was a lil travel size spray bottle with a very dark brown liquid in it. She must have passed it back to Kayla to put in her locker after she sprayed it on me. There was also a small Amazon box that was ripped open next to it. I took a look inside, and there was a bottle of coyote urine.*

*This trout mouth heifer! I took my phone out, opened up my Amazon app, and searched for coyote urine. It popped right up! She purchased the four ounce bottle for nine dollars and ninety nine cents. I opened it up and poured that revolting smelling ass liquid all over her shit, including her cell phone.*

*As I was leaving, Kayla tried to run up on me. I dropped my bag and was getting ready to gut punch that bitch, but security got in my way, once again. She would have folded like a lawn chair. I promised her I would get both of their asses back.*

I got the last laugh that night but was still feeling the effects of not being employed. Big Worm ugly ass had me banned from all the local clubs. His bitch probably told him to do that. One of the security guards I was cool with walked me to my car that night. He told me that Keema had been fucking Big Worm.

That explained why he tried to stop me from stomping her out. It was a setup. She wanted her sister to dance with her that night, not me. They wanted to stop my bag and keep it in the family. I don't think Big Worm had a part in that because I made him a lot of money. It was me laying hands on him in front of everyone that got me fired and stopped my coins.

I couldn't even collect unemployment. They considered me an independent contractor because I didn't receive an actual paycheck. Even though I filed taxes every year, I didn't pay into the system, so I couldn't collect from it.

Most of the money I saved up was almost gone because I used it to pay my bills. I didn't receive any assistance at all, but I recently applied for every damn thing. I went down to social services and signed up for anything I qualified for. They needed to approve my food stamps asap. These kids were eating me out of house and home.

My feet were pleased when I made it back home. I went into the bathroom and closed the door. As I stood in front of the mirror, I slid my momma's hat from off my head. My cheeks were a lil blush from the cold weather. The pinkish glow illuminated the freckles on them.

I turned on the faucet, splashed some warm water on my face, and grabbed a hand towel. As I collected the droplets of water, I surveyed my face. My eyebrows were overgrown and definitely needed to be done. I barely had any eyelashes, and it seemed like everyday my round, brown face got fuller.

Forcing myself to smile, I admired my teeth. They were beautiful. While staring at my reflection, my light brown eyes puffed up with tears. The tears spilled out onto my cheeks, trickled down my face, and met at my chin. My chest started to feel heavy as a lump formed in my throat.

When I sat down on the edge of the tub and leaned forward, everything I had been holding in over the last few months came crashing down on me like a ton of bricks. I felt so overwhelmed with grief and anxiety about how I was going to take care of my kids. The cry that exited my body came from the depths of my soul.

I thought my sons were still asleep until they came crashing through the bathroom door. They must have thought something happened to me. All three of them stared at me without saying a word, then hugged me at once.

My boys were the best part of me. I let them know I was fine and just had a lot on my plate, so I needed a good cry. They didn't like it when I was sad and worried about me. It hurted my heart even more that they had to see me in such a state.

After I gathered myself, we did our little secret handshake we came up with. No one was allowed to teach it to anyone else. It was only for us four. That put a smile on their faces, and it was all I needed to see. It changed my whole mood. There was no other bond like that of a mother and her sons.

We all left the bathroom and headed toward the kitchen. I needed to get breakfast started. It had been a long day already.

# Chapter Two

FIVE DAYS BEFORE VALENTINE'S DAY

DELILAH

As I laid on top of my bed and stared up at the ceiling, I wondered why life kept on punching me in the face. I just came from getting my mail and inside was a certified letter from my landlord, Mr. Herman. Nothing good came in a certified letter to your house.

Usually, someone wanted your attention and their money. I was two months behind on my rent, including this month. My dumb ass wanted my kids to have the best Christmas ever, so I spent too much money on them, when I should have paid my rent ahead.

I figured I would get back to work right after the holidays. So, I splurged, being that I had a little nest egg stashed away.

That was before finding out Big Worm had my ass flagged in all the clubs. They had my picture posted in their establishments like they do the people who steal out of Walmart. I was mad as hell when I found that out.

I didn't even want to open the letter because I already knew what it was going to say. My landlord wanted his money, and this was probably my final notice. There was no sense in me putting it off any longer. I tore open the letter and couldn't believe my eyes.

This crusty ass muthafucka sent me a notice of eviction. I had to appear before the courts in three weeks, or pay the balance in full before that time, including court cost and late fees. *How the hell am I gonna come up with all this money within three weeks?*

I would be damned if I went and begged Big Worm's warthog looking ass for my job back. I'd rather sell crack under a bridge butt naked with billy goats tied to my ass before I did that shit. Asking my momma for it was an option, but all she would do was cuss my ass out. Nobody had time for that. She'd say I needed to take everything I bought the kids back to the store. Plus, she was strapped for cash anyway from taking care of my sister and her kids.

Paying Mr. Herman a visit was my only option at this point. I'd just have to break down and do it. Hopefully, I could work out a payment plan with him to keep me from having to go to court. I owed him a total of $4,850 because he also asked for March's rent. He included it in the amount, and that was some bullshit!

I didn't understand how the court allowed them to ask for rent money in advance. That was like the cable company billing you a month ahead. The shit just ain't right, but I needed to stop complaining and go handle my business.

Mr. Herman lived in an area out of walking distance, so I was going to have to ride one of my sons' bikes. I couldn't afford to spend any money on an Uber. The last time I rode a bike I must have been their age. I hope I didn't fall and break all the bones in my body.

I got myself together and headed back outside. As soon as I sat on the bike, my whole ass swallowed up the seat. I wobbled for a little bit as I got going, but I quickly remembered what I was doing. My knees kept hitting my arms as I pedaled, but there wasn't anything I could do about that. This was about to be an uncomfortable ride.

It only took me twenty minutes to make it to my land-lord's house. I was out of breath and sweating profusely, even though it was thirty five degrees outside. After I climbed off the bike and rested it on the inside of Mr. Herman's fence, I took a couple of deep breaths while pulling the suction outta my ass.

I walked up to his house and rang the doorbell. The sound it made creeped me out. There was a gray cat in the window looking at me. I hated cats. Mr. Herman opened his door, welcoming me in.

This was the first time I had been inside his house. There was no reason for me to come here because I mailed him my rent check. That was the extent of our tenant/landlord relationship. When I called letting him know I needed to talk in person, he was more than eager to have me over.

He cleared off an area on his couch and offered me a seat. Mr. Herman was up in here living foul. There was shit everywhere. Being an older gentleman, he probably couldn't clean as well, but that wasn't an excuse. Mr. Herman owned quite a few properties in my neighborhood and needed to hire a damn cleaning service. I knew he could afford it.

He sat across from me in his recliner, licked his lips, and stared at me like I was a rump roast surrounded by potatoes and carrots, fresh out of the oven. Let me find out Mr. Herman was a chubby chaser. Now, I understood why there was no hesitation in his voice when he said I could stop by.

I'd seen him in Big Worm's Rump Shakers before. He patronized it all the time. We never interacted, though; not even a lap dance. Maybe he would have felt uncomfortable being that I was his tenant, so he never requested me.

The cat started rubbing up against my leg. I didn't even see this muthafucka jump down from the window sill. They were sneaky as hell, which was why I didn't like them. I stomped my foot, scaring it off.

"So, what can I do for you, Ms. Jones?"

He tugged at his beard that was gray just like the little bit of curly hair on top of his head. He needed to cut it all off. The shit was in patches.

"I received your certified letter today informing me that you want to kick me and my kids outta yo house. Hopefully, we can come to some sort of agreement to stop that from happening."

"Yeah, I really didn't wanna send you that. You sorta forced my hand when you didn't pay anything on your rent. Did you think you could just live over there rent free?" He stared at me waiting for an answer.

Shit, of course I didn't think I could live there for free. He never said anything to me when I missed the first month, so I figured he wasn't sweating it. I was going to pay him eventually. If anything, I should have made a good faith payment, like I did on my utility bills.

"I don't have any excuses on why I didn't contact you earlier before shit got outta hand. I've been going through a lot since I lost my job. I keep looking for other work with no success."

All I knew was dancing in the clubs. It was the only job I had as an adult. I did some clerical work as a teenager when I was in high school, but nothing else. I worked after school for a property management company all four years.

I only did that to earn me some extra cash, dancing has always been my goal. My older cousin Juicy was a dancer. She had been sneaking me into the club with her since I was sixteen. I would sit in the back of the room, watching her own the stage.

Those men, women too, would spend their whole paychecks on her ass. Just tossing money on the stage or tucking it in her bra and g-string. I watched in amazement, wanting to do the same thing one day. It was easy money, but you had to work hard to be the best at it. My cousin was very skillful, so she always collected her bag.

I practiced every weekend in my room, determined to be the best to ever do it when my turn came. Working on signature moves and dance routines, I would also have an advantage over the other girls since Juicy showed me the ropes at an early age. She eventually moved to New York to dance. She was killing it up there; living in a penthouse apartment overlooking the city. I needed to pay her a visit one day.

"I heard about you being dragged up outta Big Worm's club. That was some foul ass shit. They didn't have to do you like that." Mr. Herman interrupted my thoughts with that bull-shit he was spewing.

"Let me clarify the misinformation you have received. First of all, no one dragged me up outta nowhere. I was escorted out by security. Second of all, that slut Keema and her minion ass sister Kayla, set me up. Those jealous ass hoes wanted to be me. They couldn't, so they got rid of my ass."

I was pissed all over again. They were out there in the streets dirtying up my name.

"Well, I guess you got me straight. Don't hurt me unless it's in a good way."

Mr. Herman snickered as he held his hands up like he was surrendering. His nasty ass was smiling hard as hell, showing all his dentures.

"And what's a good way to hurt you?" I questioned Mr. Herman as I unzipped my coat, bit down on my bottom lip, and got comfortable on the couch. I saw exactly where his old, horny ass was going. I figured I would play right along with his raunchy ass. If I had to get down in the mud with him, so be it.

"Do you mind if I take off my coat? It's getting a lil warm, and I'm starting to heat up."

He didn't say a word. Mr. Herman shook his head no while watching my every move. I slowly removed my coat, like I was undressing for him.

I had on one of my good bras from Lane Bryant, so it's holding everything in place. I adjusted them on purpose, making them jiggle. Mr. Herman gazed at me like he was watching a peep show. He wiped the slob that dribbled out of the side of his mouth with the back of his hand, then wiped it on his pants. Yuck!

"Now back to my question. How would you like for me to hurt you... in a good way?"

I batted my eyes at him while speaking in a seductive tone.

"Anyway you want. I'm open to all suggestions." He smiled like a Cheshire Cat.

"What's in it for me? I have some suggestions but need to know that I will still have a place to call home after I put this good hurting on you. Know what I'm saying?"

Mr. Herman must be out his fucking mind if he thought for one second that I was doing anything with him for free.

"Depending on how good of a hurting you put on me, I'm willing to reduce what you owe me by $1,000."

"A $1,000!" I yelled, making him jump.

"I'm willing to negotiate."

"We need to be clear on what exactly it is you expect me to do to you. Are we talking about a private dance here or something else?"

"Yes, I think a private dance would be sufficient. I need to be able to touch you, though, and for it to last at least an hour."

I guess the thought of it had him aroused. His monkey ass was sitting over there with an erection, and I could tell Mr. Herman was working with a little something, something from the way it was poking.

"What would it take for you to wipe my debt clean, and stop the eviction altogether?" I had nothing to lose at this point, so I was willing to do whatever it took to keep a roof over my kids' head. The way Mr. Herman undressed me with his eyes, I knew he would be willing to go further.

"Spend Valentine's Day with me. I want the whole experience. Do everything to me as if I was your man. And don't worry about me keeping up, my blue buddy here will make sure I can."

I didn't know whether to be offended by the fact he assumed I didn't have plans for Valentine's Day already, or to be appalled by him shaking his bottle of viagra at me.

I could see he didn't have a problem getting it up. Staying that way must have been his issue. If bouncing on someone's pop pop kept me and my kids in our home, let the rodeo begin! I fucked on niggas for less before.

"You have a deal. I'm gonna need you to put it in writing, though. You can leave out the particulars. I just need some sorta receipt from you stating that I have a zero balance. One more thing. We're doing this at my house. There's no way in hell I'm laying up in here."

My face has the look of disgust written all over it as my words left my lips. This bat cave he called a home looked more like the Munsters lived here than an old man and his cat. A layer of dust, about a half of an inch thick, was on everything. Cobwebs adorned every corner, and random shit was just scattered all over. Stacks of books were everywhere. They look like they haven't been read in twenty years. I actually felt bad for Mr. Herman. He must have been lonely. No wonder he was always in the clubs.

"I will write you a receipt right now, but will give it to you after our night has come to an end. Sit tight while I go get my receipt book out the kitchen."

As he exited the room, I grabbed my coat to put it back on. The damn cat jumped out from underneath it, scaring the shit out of me. I had to hurry up and get the hell out of here. This cat was trying to kill me. I gave my coat a good shake before putting it on.

Glancing around the room, I noticed a picture of a handsome, young man that resembled Mr. Herman. I went over and picked the picture up to get a better look at him.

Mr. Herman wasn't ugly, just old. You could tell he was a catch back in the day. He had big, dark brown eyes, honey colored skin like me, and a large nose that fitted his face perfectly. If he threw some vaseline across those thick, cracked lips of his, they might be kissable.

"Is this you?" I questioned Mr. Herman when he came back into the room.

"No, that's my son Darius. I have a daughter too. She lives out on the West Coast." Darius' ass was fine as hell. I didn't even know Mr. Herman had kids. They must not visit a lot. "He just retired from the Air Force. He entered straight outta high school and served for twenty years. Now, he was coming home to take over my business. I'm getting too old for this shit. Matter of fact, he should be here sometime this weekend. He's driving up from Virginia. I think he's about a six hour drive from New Jersey."

"Hopefully, I'll get to meet my new landlord." I chuckled, putting the picture back down.

"In due time. Meanwhile, I will see you on Valentine's Day. How does six o'clock sound?" He had a lil pep in his step now.

"That's fine with me. I will hang out with my kids in the morning and see you that night."

I can't believe I was really doing this shit. Mr. Herman walked me out and stood on the porch as I climbed back on my son's bike. I wasn't looking forward to this ride home and neither was my ass.

"Don't forget to prepare the purple bag, Jaws," Mr. Herman yelled as I started to ride away.

All I could do was give his old ass the finger as I tried to keep from falling off the damn bike.

# Chapter Three

FOUR DAYS BEFORE VALENTINE'S DAY

DELILAH

I was at home getting me and my kids ready to go over to my mom's house for dinner. She made us gather together every holiday, no matter which one, and I wished she would stop. Every time we were all in the same room some bullshit kicked off. We always ended up like the scenes in *Welcome Home Roscoe Jenkins*; arguing, fighting and tearing shit up.

We were each responsible for bringing a dish or two, but it seemed like it was always just my mom and I who did all the cooking. Denise had to bring the paper products each time with her non cooking ass. I guarantee you she won't go buy a thing now that she stayed there.

Fried chicken and potato salad were the two dishes I agreed

to bring. I liked to fry my chicken hard. It came out nice and crispy too. I coated it in flour, then dipped it into an egg mixture, making sure it was completely covered. After the egg mixture, I coated it in flour again.

The key to making sure that skin got crispy was frying it in piping hot grease. If that grease wasn't hot, the chicken would just soak up the oil. No one will eat that shit. It belonged in a biohazard bag.

I always made my potato salad the day before, so it could do a situation marination in the fridge. Besides eggs, relish, celery, onion, a squirt of mustard, and mayonnaise, I would put a pinch of sugar in it to balance out the salt. The same way if you made something sweet, add a pinch of salt to balance out the sweetness.

Both my dishes were ready and sitting on the table by the door. My mom was going to swing by and pick us up. There was no way I could carry all this food over there. I made two half pans of each dish. I made extra, so she didn't have to cook for a few days.

These kids needed to hurry up and get ready before she got here. If my mom had to beep twice for us to come out, we wouldn't hear the end of it.

"Alright, sons, I'm gonna need y'all to put a lil pep in y'all step. I don't wanna hear Big Mama's mouth!" I knew they were moving like tortoises because they didn't want to go either.

They always ended up arguing with their cousins, Denise's annoying ass kids. Her daughters always picked with my sons. Those little muthafuckas liked to put their hands on people, but I told my sons not to hit them back. My nieces are seven and nine, so they were big enough to know better. If they tried that shit today, I was going to get their asses.

I put on my coat and grabbed my mom's hat to give back to her. I threw a few braids in my hair last night, so my holiday wig could make its appearance. Since she only came out a few times a year, Cayenne was in excellent condition. She was jet black, shoulder length, wavy, and spicy.

**Beep!**

"Come on, sons! Big Mama is here. Let's roll out."

They came rushing out of their rooms fully dressed. I opened the door while they put their stuff on, so she could see we were ready. I said a quick prayer, asking the universe to cover us because we were gonna need it.

————

"Hang up y'all coats, then go wash y'all hands." I ordered my kids.

We were the first to arrive. Denise came out dressed like she was going to a ball. She wore a floor length, red fitted dress, a pearl necklace, and some stilettos.

She always had a nice shape. I would give her that. Even after having both her kids, she just bounced back. All I did was bounce after having mine.

Meanwhile, I looked like I was going to the laundromat. I had on a black Nike sweatsuit and all black Nike sneakers. The only thing classy on me was Cayenne. Denise looked me up and down like I was for sale.

"Hey, Dee. Glad you guys could make it tonight. It's always

good to see you and my nephews." Denise sarcastically greeted me.

This bitch was acting like it was her house. She already had a drink in her hand. If it was that cheap ass gin, we were all in trouble tonight.

"Yeah, we made it. I'm happy to see y'all as well. Let me go help mom. I'll get back witcha."

I hated the sight of that cackling cow. She terrorized my ass when we were growing up and still fucked with me now. Denise always thought she was better than me.

We were sisters, but it never felt like it. She turned everything into a competition between us. Denise had to be the best and have all the attention. If I drew momma a picture with crayons and gave it to my mom, she would paint ten to give to her. Stupid shit like that.

Denise sought out to humiliate me every chance she got too. She embarrassed me in front of her friends by calling me out of my name. One time she even whipped my ass in front of them. Denise was three years older than me and stronger back then. She stayed putting her hands on me. I liked to see her try that shit now.

"Mom, what do you need me to do?"

She mumbled under her breath, so I knew someone pissed her off already.

"Check the candy yams that are in the oven. Tell the boys to take the food that's already done into the dining room and put it on the table. Your sister's useless ass didn't help do shit. She's too busy dressing up to go to the living room. Her monkey ass thinks she's Diana muthafuckin' Ross." My mom continued to fuss and cuss as I did what I was told.

It was her fault Denise acted the way she did. Our mom always coddled her. I knew she favored her, but my mom won't admit it. Every time Denise was about to fall flat on her face, she came to her rescue. How could Denise succeed in this life if she didn't know what it felt like to fail?

This wasn't the first time Denise had been evicted. She knew our mom would always let her come stay, so she never cared about anything and took no responsibility for herself or her actions. Denise would quit jobs like Tichina Arnold in *Everybody Hates Chris*, but she ain't got no husband to fall back on, and her man was in jail.

As I put the place settings down on the table, the front door swung open. It was my uncle Junebug. I don't even think I knew his real name. That was what we always called him my whole life. He was my mom's only brother and one of my favorite people. Uncle Junebug had the paper products.

"Uncle Junebug!" I rushed over to hug him.

Last time we were together was on Christmas. My boys were right behind me, hugging him too. They loved him so much. He gave them ten dollars each time he saw them.

"Now, y'all put that away, so those Bebe's kids don't see it. I'm not giving Denice's offspring a damn thing." They said thank you, then tucked the money away in their pockets.

"Don't tell them that." I tapped my uncle on his shoulder. "Boys, go in the room with your auntie and cousins."

I laughed so hard I could barely get my words out. Uncle

Junebug didn't get along with Denise either. I wasn't aware he had issues with her kids too, damn.

"She moved back in with y'all mom, and I'm pissed. That girl knows she's a user. Denise can't stand me because I call her out on her shit."

"What did her kids do to you, though? Why didn't you wanna give them any money?" Uncle Junebug had it to give, so that couldn't be the reason. He has a good ass job, no kids, and saved all his cash.

I could ask him for the rent money I owed, but I didn't want him to know I was struggling. He had always been so proud of the way I grinded for me and my sons. He wasn't fond of the fact that I danced, but respected my hustle. I never wanted him to view me differently.

"Those little crumb snatchers stole money outta my wallet on Christmas. I left it on the kitchen counter by accident, so I went back in there to go get it. Don't you know Heckle and Jeckle were in there splitting my shit." I cried real tears at this point. All I could see were two black birds digging in his wallet.

"I smacked my hand down on the kitchen table, startling the lil criminals. They threw the wallet and money back on the counter. I started to pluck their eye sockets loose but told Denise instead, and she ain't do a damn thing." Uncle Junebug's mouth was tight as hell telling the story. He spoke through clenched teeth.

"That's a damn shame. Uf they steal from me, I will beat their asses... and hers too if she doesn't like it. They're too young to be stealin', especially from family." I shook my head.

Uncle Junebug headed into the kitchen to say hello to my mom. Denise came back out to make herself another drink, pouring up that cheap ass gin. She had to tell our mom to buy that specifically for her. No one else drank that shit. I took a sip one time, just to see how it tasted, and it felt like someone held a blowtorch up to my throat.

"You can have the kids come out. We're ready to sit down and eat," I informed her.

The kids' table was already set up when I got here. I just finished up the adult table now.

"Everything looks so nice. You're so domestic. Maybe you should consider becomin' a maid since you not dancin' anymore," Denise joked, but I didn't find shit funny.

This bitch came for me every chance she got. I bit my lip so hard I could taste blood. My mom was running her mouth again about me.

"And you should consider going down to the SPCA. I'm sure there is a family looking to adopt a pet. You would make a great guard dog." She started it, and I was going to finish it.

We yelled insults back and forth at each other until our mom came out of the kitchen swinging a dish towel. She stood in the middle and put her hands up, trying to separate us.

"Stop this foolishness right now! I'm sick of y'all not getting along. When is this bullshit gonna stop? Y'all scaring the damn kids!" I didn't even notice that they came out of the room and were standing there watching.

"Kids, come sit down to eat. Y'all mommas we're just playing." Uncle Junebug instructed them as he gave me the *come here* look. I followed him into the kitchen.

"She sets the trap, and you get caught in it every time. I didn't even have to hear or see what happened to know she started it. You have to learn to ignore her ass." He opened the fridge and grabbed us each a beer.

"You right. I'm just tired of the insults."

I twisted the cap off and took a sip. It was nice and cold and exactly what I needed.

"Look at who they are comin' from. Her words don't hold no weight. Denise is miserable as hell right now. Don't let her transfer her negative energy to you, baby girl."

"It's hard when you in the moment. I've been suckin' up shit from her for years." I could feel the tears threatening to fall.

"You better than this is all I'm sayin'."

Uncle Junebug gave me a hug, and we went back into the living room. My mom was already making the kids' plates, so I helped her out. Once they were situated, I sat down at the table in between her and my uncle.

"Mom, I thought you said Auntie Vera wasn't comin'?" I questioned.

"She's not comin'," she replied, rolling her eyes towards Denise.

"So why did you add an extra place settin'?"

I only set one for each of us and now, there was one more next to my sister.

"That's for Denise's friend that's supposed to be comin'.

He's late and was responsible for the ice and drinks," she replied.

Uncle Junebug let out a long sigh. I didn't even respond to my mom. I just bit into that good chicken I fried.

Denice didn't help cook, set up, or feed her own damn kids. I couldn't believe she had the nerve to invite a guest. No wonder she looked like she was about to walk the red carpet.

"I wish Vera was comin'. She usually brings the dessert. I'm gonna miss that peach cobbler." Uncle Junebug chimed in as he licked his lips. My boys were too. They loved anything she made.

The kids were quiet. They were throwing down and watching a movie my mom put on the TV for them. It kept them from arguing with each other for the moment.

"Do you have a date for Valentine's Day, Dee?" Denise asked out of nowhere.

This bitch really wanted to test me tonight.

"Yes, I do, Denise."

I forced myself to smile when I really wanted to smack the piss out of her.

"I'm not talkin' about my nephews." Denise laughed. "I mean a *real* date."

She wasn't going to stop until I whipped her ass. Uncle Junebug shook his head no at me while shoving a forkful of collard greens into his mouth.

"Mom, do you mind keepin' the boys on Valentine's Day for me, so I can have my *real* date?" She nodded her head yes.

"Good for you. I guess you have time to date now since they fired you from the club." Denise sneered.

She took another sip of that liquid courage that was about to get her head knocked off her shoulders. Denise mentioned me not working again on purpose. I guess she wanted our uncle to know about it, or was trying to bait me once again.

"You're not workin'? Why didn't you tell me?" Uncle Junebug questioned.

He stared at me, waiting for an answer. I could see the confusion and hurt in his eyes. Uncle Junebug was caught off guard by her words, and I became enraged.

"Why don't you mind ya muthafuckin' business, bitch! Yo man is in jail, meanwhile yo lil friend is on his way over here. Worry about that shit right there, and the fact that you had to move in with our mom, once again. You triflin' ass whore."

"Yo kids' father is the reason he's in jail, and from what mom told me, we're 'bout to be roommates. You barely holdin' on by a thread, so it's only a matter of time before yo ass is kicked out into the streets. Maybe you shouldn't throw stones when you live in a glass house."

Why she told Denise my business when she knew her ass would use it against me, was beyond my comprehension. It felt intentional at this point, but I would deal with my mom later.

"No, you have that backwards. My sons' father is in jail 'cause your weak ass baby daddy snitched. Why you think his punk ass only got eight years when he was facing thirty? His name is on everyone's paperwork, you dirty ass trick. You know his ass ain't nothin' but a snake."

Our kids' fathers used to be best friends. They did everything together, including getting money. Her baby daddy started fucking with a different connect. My sons' father, who was my man at the time, didn't trust it. He wanted to stick with who they always dealt with.

He felt saving a few dollars wasn't worth the risk, so they severed their business relationship, but remained friends. They both still got to the bag, but my man just kept things flowing the way it always was.

Denise's man didn't know his new connect was working with the feds. Once they showed him all the evidence they had against him, he became an informant in order to reduce his time. That bastard sang like a canary. She was lucky he still had breath in his body.

"Trick? You just mad 'cause you don't look like me. Sittin' there looking like a 200 pound bag of russet potatoes with yo ol' recyclin' bin body havin' ass." She always tried to come for my weight.

"I'm tellin' both you heifers to stop right the fuck now!" My momma barked as she closed her eyes like she was about to say a prayer.

"Naw, let 'em get this shit off their chest. This is yo fault anyway." Uncle Junebug pointed at my mom. He looked back over at me. "Imma 'bout to get these kids into the room, and y'all gonna hash this shit out."

Uncle Junebug got up from the table and had the kids take their food with them into the bedroom.

"How is any of this my fault?" My mom questioned her

brother when he returned to the table.

"Don't play dumb, Sis. I will tell you 'bout yo'self later. Meanwhile, y'all continue. Say what you have to say now 'cause once you do, that's it! This shit stops today."

I'd been waiting for this opportunity my whole life! Every time I got ready to tear into Denice's ass, my mom always came to her rescue. Now that I had the floor, it was time to mop her ass with it.

"Don't nobody wanna look like yo fake Viola Davis lookin' ass. All dressed up with nowhere to go. And you can call me fat all you want. My belly may be in my lap when I'm sittin' down, but good pussy needs extra protection. Ask yo baby daddy. I had to protect it from him." Denise's eyes almost popped out of her head. "When he was out, he stayed in the club tryna get me into the champagne room. I'm not a savage like you, though. If I was, I woulda been his *fifth* baby momma!" I smirked.

My sister slept with anyone who gave me any attention. She hated my confidence with her insecure ass and tried to destroy it every chance she got. That shit affected me when I was younger but now, I didn't give a fuck! I loved all of me; every bump, dimple, stretch mark, and roll.

"He never wanted yo stank ass. The only people who want you are the old, dusty ass men who toss their social security checks on yo ass cheeks. You thought you were the baddest bitch, now you the brokest bitch. Do you need me to give you a ride home since they repoed yo car? Pretty soon yo sons are gonna have to hit the block like their daddy did to help you out. Now smirk at that!" Denise cut her eyes at me.

This hoe probably didn't have enough gas to give me a ride next door. She stayed driving on E with her check engine light on, but she fucked up mentioning my kids.

And once again, my momma played both sides. She talked about me to Denise, then would talk about her to me. That was why Uncle Junebug told my momma it was her fault. But like he said, she wanted to play dumb.

"Naw, I don't need a ride." I smiled. "But I will ride with you back to Planned Parenthood, so you can get yo other kids you left there in the dumpster. Did you tell ya momma you've been getting abortions ever since you were sixteen? And please don't forget to tell her about all the STDs you done had. I'm surprised yo pussy is still holdin' on and hasn't dropped into yo panties yet."

"Alright now, that's enough! Y'all hitting below the belt, and I'm not listening to this shit any more." My mom was almost in tears.

She created this monster, and now she wanted to cry. Denise glared at me.

"Mom, this is what I mean. You let her call me names, disrespect me, and play in my face but as soon as I'm ripping her a new one, you heard enough? Everyone knows she's your favorite. I believe you love both of us, but you like her more than me... you always have. I had to live in her shadow my entire life. You forced me to fly early while allowin' her to stay in the nest longer. It's fucked up, and it hurts."

As soon as I finished talking, a pan of barbecue chicken came flying at me. I threw up my hands to block my face. Before

Denise could grab something else to throw at me, I was already up and around to her side of the table.

I snatched Denise by her hair, slid one of the pans of my mac and cheese over, and pushed her whole face in it. Then I snatched the bitch up from her seat. My mom tried to pull me off of her, but I had a death grip on her braids. I heard my uncle tell my mom to let me go.

If she wasn't my sister, I would have beat Denise's ass silly. Instead, I just shook her head a few times, hard as hell, then slammed her to the ground. I turn around, focusing my eyes on my mom.

"You wrong! Why you pulling on me like she didn't just toss a pan of chicken in my face? She put her hands on me for years growin' up, and you did nothing about it. The one time I defend myself, you only grab me. Like I said, you don't treat us the same. I'm getting my kids, and we ain't neva comin' back as long as she is here."

My mom just stood there with her hand over her mouth, looking appalled. She acted as if everything I just said was a lie.

I went into the bathroom to clean myself up. It felt like I wanted to cry but the tears just wouldn't fall. As I washed my hands, I could see Uncle Junebug through the mirror. He stood there with his arms open. I laid my head on his chest, and he wrapped his arms around me. The tears easily escaped my eyes at that point.

My uncle didn't say a word. He just allowed me to release years of hurt that finally came to the surface. Now, the healing process could begin because I finally told my mom how I felt. I'd been holding this pain inside since I was a child.

"You need me to give y'all a ride home?" he asked.

"We good. The walk and fresh air will give me time to relax my mind before I get home."

When I went to the bedroom to tell my sons we were leaving, I opened the door and heard my youngest niece say to my kids that I was a fat ass.

"What's goin' on in here?" They all looked up at me.

"We heard y'all yelling and opened the door. You were beating up Aunt Denise. They got mad and started calling you names and making fun of you 'cause you a little fat." My oldest son looked sad. "I said you not that big and at least you don't look like a man. Then she poked me in the eye." His left eye was red.

"Which one poked you?" He pointed to my oldest niece.

I pinched my niece right on the meaty part under her arm with all my strength. She started crying, but I didn't care. I told my kids to get their shit. Denice could clean up the mess in this room.

As we were headed out, Denise asked why her daughter was crying. We kept right on walking out the door, ignoring her ass. I warned my nieces before about putting their hands on my sons. Fuck all of them at this point.

"Excuse me. Is this Denice's house? My GPS sent me on a goose chase trying to find the place. I'm so freaking late."

This poindexter looking ass dude questioned me as we

walked down the steps. He was holding a bag of melting ice and a case of root beer soda.

"This is my mom's house, but Denise is staying here because she was evicted. Her man will be getting outta jail soon, so be careful. And make sure you wrap it up because she's a hot box thot. Enjoy!" I whispered in his ear.

It was cold as hell outside, but my sons didn't mind. They were laughing and joking around with each other as we walked home. I started thinking about my Valentine's Day date with Mr. Herman. *Who's gonna watch my boys now?*

# Chapter Four

THREE DAYS BEFORE VALENTINE'S DAY

DELILAH

The next morning, I was sitting in my living room, folding laundry, when I got a phone call from my mom. She wanted to come over so we could talk. I really don't have shit to say to her or my sister. My uncle probably tore into her ass, making her feel guilty. That was the only reason she wanted to come and say her peace. I knew her like the back of my hand.

I told her she could stop on by. She better not be coming over here to tell me I was wrong. If she did, I would politely ask her to leave. Either way, I needed her to watch my kids, so I can get this rent paid. It was wrong of me to say they couldn't go back over to her house.

She always watched them, and I could honestly say she didn't treat them any different from Denise's kids. I was grateful she was a better grandmother than she was a mother. My boys loved going to her house. Matter of fact, she could take them back with her. I needed the next couple days to be alone, so I could get myself and this house ready for Valentine's Day.

"Morning, Dee. How are you doin'?" My mother greeted me as I let her into the house.

"Morning, mom, I'm good. Just in here doing laundry while the boys are on their video games. How are you?"

"A lot better now that I get to talk to you. I didn't sleep at all last night. After you left, Uncle Junebug let my ass have it. He was livid. I've never seen him so upset in all my life. He felt like I always chose Denise over you."

"That's because you do. You the only one who can't see it. Or don't want to." Maybe she wasn't aware of what she was doing. I was just glad someone else told her, so she wouldn't think I was making the shit up.

"You both were right, but I didn't realize it until I heard the words roll off your lips. I saw the hurt in your eyes when you looked at me. Then when your uncle confirmed it, I had to take a deeper look at myself."

"I never thought I would hear those words." She was sincere too. I could tell she meant what she was saying.

"Dee, I apologize for making' you feel less than. It's not true, but now I understand why you felt that way. You are the stronger one. You've always been so confident in who you are. I didn't think you needed me as much as she did. I was wrong for that."

My mother held my hands as she delivered me the apology I always wanted. I needed to hear those words. Parents sometimes forget that the strong ones need nurturing too. We shouldn't be punished for being responsible or sure of ourselves.

"I appreciate you for recognizin' where you fell short. I accept your apology. Hopefully, one day Denise and I can work out our differences. I don't see that happenin' anywhere in the near future, but one day."

"That child needs to get her shit together and get up outta my house. Her kids don't listen. She just lets them run wild. The oldest one said you pinched her."

I burst out laughing. My momma joined in, and I laughed so hard my cheeks started hurting.

"She's damn right I pinched her ass. I warned her, and her sinister sister, about puttin' their hands on my sons. They know they're not gonna hit them back, so they take advantage. I had enough of everyone's shit last night."

"Well, let me get back home before they burn my house down. They already overflowed my toilet using too much damn tissue. It's like they wrap their hand up in a cast before they tear it off. You can hear the damn toilet paper roll spinning 'round and 'round when they are in there. We go through a roll a day."

That's what she gets for letting them back in. I would have taken the kids and let Denise go to a shelter. My mom was going to have a stroke messing around with them.

"Oh yeah, mom, can the boys go with you for the next few

days? I really do have someone comin' over for Valentine's Day. It will be so much easier to get this house, and myself, together if I don't have to keep cleanin' up behind them. I will pick 'em up that morning, then drop 'em back that afternoon."

"You know you don't have to ask. And I'm glad to see you finally gettin' to have some fun yourself."

While I told the boys to pack their bags, my phone rang. It was Mr. Herman. He said his ass got admitted into the hospital after he tripped over the damn cat and fell down the steps, breaking his hip.

He wanted to postpone the date until he was better but said I could come to the hospital, and he would give me my receipt. Mr. Herman had one of the EMTs grab it on their way out. My mom would have to drop me off.

—————

I had my visitor's pass in my hand as I walked around, trying to find Mr. Herman's room. It smelled like disinfectant and dirty socks up in here. After touring half the damn floor, I arrived at his room. The door was closed, so I knocked before entering.

"Delilah, is that you?" Mr. Herman asked.

"Yes, it's me," I replied while coming into his view.

He didn't have a roommate, but had the dividing curtain drawn. I guess he didn't want you to open the door and stare him right in the face.

"Come sit down and rest your feet. I hope you didn't ride that bike up here. I noticed you didn't have a car when you came over to my house." He was all up in my damn business.

"No, I caught a ride. How the hell did you fall over the cat? They're usually quick moving animals."

He probably was drunk. I could smell the bourbon on his breath when I was at his house the other day.

"I was heading up the steps to go to bed when she rushed past me chasing after something. She startled me, I lost my footing, and fell down all the steps. I was almost to the top when it happened."

Mr. Herman fell down all those steps because his equilibrium was already off kilter. I'm glad he didn't break his damn neck. He was a tall man, so that was a hard, long fall.

"I'm mad as hell! I wanted you to give me the best lap dance of your life. Now, I have to go into surgery tomorrow, so I will have to dream about it instead. Unless you want to pull the curtain back again, and do a lil shimmy for me." He raised his eyebrows a few times, then licked his lips.

"I know you muthafuckin' lyin'. Absolutely not! You're banged up, laying in here on pain meds. The sight of one of my titties will raise your blood pressure through the roof. If I give you a preview of this roller coaster ride, you'll fuck around and have a heart attack. Yo kids aren't gonna blame me for putting yo ass six feet under."

As soon as I said that, the door swung open. In walked the fine ass man from the picture, Mr. Herman's son. My body started to heat up, and I had to cross my feet and squeeze my knees together. I haven't felt this way about a man since I was with my ex.

His ass had been in jail for the last four years. That's how long it's been since I had some. I knew Darius could knock the cobwebs and dust off my pussy if given the opportunity. I chewed on my bottom lip as I surveyed him from top to bottom.

He was definitely over six feet and had the same eyes as his daddy, with a broad nose, thick lips, and hooded eyes. His eyebrows were perfect. I was a lil bit jealous of them. Darius was the color of dark brown sugar. I wondered if he tasted just as sweet.

"Hey, son! When did you get here?" Mr. Herman's face lit up like fireworks in the sky.

"I just got into town. I came straight here once you told me what happened."

Darius glanced over at me and smiled, revealing dimples in both cheeks.

*Sheesh, can he get any finer?*

"This here is Delilah. She's one of our tenants and was my Valentine's Day date, until Smokey tried to kill me."

Now he knew damn well it wasn't Smokey. It was Jack... Jack Daniel's. And why did he just announce my business like that right from the gate?

"Nice to make your acquaintance, Ms. Delilah. Such a lovely name for a beautiful, young lady."

I wanted to salute him with both hands, then rub them all over his body.

"Thank you. It's such a pleasure to meet you as well."

I wanted to say so much more; all of it inappropriate of course.

"Did I hear correctly that you were my father's date?" Darius stared at me with a confused look on his face.

"Yeah, you heard correctly. I'm gonna take all nine lives out of Smokey's ass for fucking this up for me."

Mr. Herman was pissed, but I was relieved. He would be in rehab for weeks. This date wasn't happening any time soon. Hopefully, I could just pay him back by the time he healed and came home.

"No disrespect to you, dad, but she's half your age. What were you gonna do with all that?" Darius laughed.

"What's funny? You think I'm too old to pull a young honey like this? I still got it, you know." Mr. Herman twisted up his lips.

"Umm, yeah, actually. And I wasn't aware that you were putting yourself back out there again." He raised his eyebrow at his dad. "Now, you left her without a date."

"Yeah, and I'm devastated behind it," I lied.

"Well, how about I take my father's place?"

Darius winked at me, and I felt flush all over. Obviously, he was just as forceful and outspoken as his dad. Darius wasted no time shooting his shot.

"Take my place! Where? In hell? Because that's where you can go if you think I'm gonna agree to that shit." Mr. Herman looked up at his son like he wanted to fight.

"You're in no condition to go, so why should she have her plans ruined? I'm sure she wouldn't mind."

"I wouldn't mind at all. Nope. I'm fine wit' it. Absolutely, fine wit' it." I couldn't chime in fast enough.

No way was I letting this opportunity slip through my fingers. This man was fine as wine and dripped sex appeal. I was ready to arch my back right for him.

"We had a deal, Delilah. You still owe me!" Mr. Herman barked.

He must have lost his rabbit ass mind, yelling at me like that. If he didn't calm down, they would be performing another surgery to get my foot out of his ass.

"Deal? What sort of deal? What are you talking about, Pops?" Darius looked perplexed.

"And I'm still holding up my end of it. I agreed to spend Valentine's Day with my landlord. Your son is technically my landlord now. You said it yourself that he was coming home to take over the family business." I could tell by the look on Darius's face he was still confused.

"Y'all had some type of arrangement?" He quizzed, pointing between the both of us.

"I agreed to this date wit' yo father in order to stop my eviction. I lost my job, fell behind on my rent, and he was about to put me and my kids out. If I spent the evening with him, yo father agreed to wipe the slate clean. That's basically it in a nutshell."

Embarrassment was written all over my face. Darius must have thought I was an irresponsible person and a horrible mother to allow myself to get in such a predicament.

"He doesn't know shit about being a landlord." Mr. Herman's ass was still on fire. His mouth was all turned up with a scowl on his face as he continued to glare at his son.

"No, but I know everything about being a gentleman. You taught me that, Pops. Plus, it would be good for me to get to know one of our tenants. Ms. Delilah can help me get back acquainted with the neighborhood. I'm sure a lot has changed since I've been gone."

I'd show him the hood alright. Right what's underneath *my* hood. He could be my mechanic and get this engine roaring again!

"You can call me Dee, and the date was to take place at my house. We had plans to stay in and hang out, but I can show you around another day, since you are back here for good. I hope that doesn't change your mind about you takin' yo father's place."

Judging from that wide ass smile across his face, he was quite pleased with staying in.

"It doesn't change a thing. I'm looking forward to our date." He licked his lips like he was L. L. Cool J.

I could see he was nasty just like his daddy. If I didn't get out of there, I would have given Darius the preview his father wanted.

"Since we're all squared away, I'm gonna leave, so y'all can have some quality time together. I hope your surgery goes well, Mr. Herman, and I'm sorry that our date didn't go as planned." I cleared my throat. "But I need that receipt, so I can put it up. Please do not forget to have your son notify the courthouse. I don't need the sheriffs rolling up to my house, trying to put me out."

I got up to leave, envelope in hand, and walked up to

Darius, taking in his scent. There was nothing better than a good smelling man to get your juices flowing.

"I'll be seeing you again, very soon. Yo father has my address and all my information. Six o'clock sharp will be a good time for you to stop by on Valentine's Day."

I tooted my lips up at him and walked away. And yes, I glanced back to see if he was watching me walk away, and he was.

*Chapter Five*

TWO DAYS BEFORE VALENTINE'S DAY

DELILAH

W*here the hell is it?*

I searched all over this house for my purple bag, looking everywhere I thought it could be, but it wasn't here. All my soul snatching items were in there, which included stuff I ordered online and picked up from different places over the years. I couldn't make a whole new bag by Valentine's Day.

The only thing that made sense was that I must have left it at Big Worm's Rump Shakers the day they escorted me out. If Keema and Kayla got their hands on my bag, it would be gone forever. They wouldn't know what to do with the shit in there and probably threw it out.

With no other option available to me, I decided to go and find my bag. If I rode that bike there and back, they would find my ass sprawled out in the middle of the road, looking like a groundhog who didn't make it across the street. Using my momma's car was my only choice.

————

I pulled up to the club and parked in the back. There weren't that many cars out there, which was good just in case I had to show my ass. Usually I entered through the side door, but since I wasn't still working there, I went through the front like everybody else.

As soon as I walked in, Kayla was up on the stage percolating. Fuck make it rain, they weren't even making it drizzle on her ass. It was more like a sprinkle. Kayla danced like my mom pulled out her stun gun and wouldn't stop shocking her ass.

I headed over to the bar and asked Trixie if Big Worm was in. I didn't want to go straight to the back. He might have called security to escort me out again. Then I would have to elbow him in the other titty. I didn't come to fight. All I wanted was my bag, so I could be on my way.

"He's in his office. I will go get him. Do you want a drink while you wait? It's on the house."

Trixie was the best bartender and always made sure the bottles kept flowing when I danced for a V.I.P. She would only send over top notch liquor, then convince them to order more shit. I would always hit her off with a nice tip at the end of the night.

"Yes, Malibu, thanks." She poured the shot and slid it over

to me, then disappeared to the back,

Big Worm came out waddling behind Trixie. I guess he said I could keep my crazy ass out on the floor where everyone could see me. He knew I was harmless, though. I'd worked here for years with no issues. That shit his bitch pulled triggered me.

"I'm glad you're here. I wanted to call you, but I didn't think you would answer. I owe you an apology for trying to hold you back. The shit Keema and Kayla did was fucked up, and I did suspend both of them after I found out. I also had them take your photo down in the other clubs and remove the ban."

Now, this walrus wanted to apologize to me. He could have come by my house if that was the case. His apology was just as fake as that cheap ass swap meet jewelry he had on. Big Worm knew damn well he didn't suspend either one of them hoes. His pockets were just feeling the effects of my departure.

As much as I could use the money, I refused to work for him ever again. This knock kneed muthafucka had me thrown out like I was trash. He banned me from dancing elsewhere, stopping me from making money to take care of me and my kids. I was about to let old ass Mr. Herman fuck on me just to cover my rent!

"It was fucked up, but there's nothing I can do about it now. I'm not here to ask for my job back. I couldn't find my purple bag and wanted to look in the locker room for it. If you could be so kind as to let me do so, I would appreciate it." I was trying really hard to be nice.

On the outside, I was laughing and smiling. On the inside, I was burning up. I wanted to punch him on top of his head like Whac-A-Mole. Kicking his kneecaps out the back of his legs would have brought me so much joy, but I *needed* my bag!

"Go on and check to see if it's back there. It's been a minute since you've been here, so I doubt it's there if you did leave it. Please don't pour any more animal piss on anything. It took us a week to air that locker room out. That was some funky ass shit."

It probably spilled right onto that dirty ass carpet he needed to pull up any damn way.

"Yeah, whateva."

When I made it to the locker room, I searched all over the place and couldn't find my purple bag. One of these hoes probably took it. I couldn't recall if security grabbed it from me or not. After I got dressed, I knew I had my bag because I put my outfit in it.

As I tried to replay the moments of that night in my head, Keema came out of the restroom. I knew she was somewhere around here once I saw her sister. It took everything in me not to beat her ass like Diamond did Ronnie in *The Players Club*.

She was lucky I didn't want to spend Valentine's Day in jail and miss out on my date with Darius' sexy ass. Plus, I had three sons at home that needed me. She wasn't worth it. Her karma was coming. This whole damn establishment would crumble. They all would reap what they sowed.

"I see someone has been eating good since she stopped dancing," Keema jeered while putting lotion on her hands and crusty ass elbows.

"And I see someone is still gnawin' on Nylabone dog chews and eating Milk-Bone treats. Did Kayla walk you before she got on stage to shake what yo momma didn't give her?"

This bitch must have forgotten who she was talking to. I was always quick with my tongue.

"That was cute what you did, pouring the coyote urine all over my shit. You're lucky you were already tossed outta here before I found out. I would have rolled your fat ass outside like a bowling ball." She cracked both sides of her neck, like she was about to do something.

"Well, you're used to markin' your territory. I just wanted to help you out that night. You started it anyway, with yo ignorant ass. Fuck you and the rest of your dog pound."

"Fuck you, the horse you rode in this muthafucka on, and ya kids. Bi—"

Before she could say another word, I rushed her ass like a linebacker for the Philadelphia Eagles. I slammed into her body like a freight train traveling at full speed, crashing her into the lockers.

Keema fell to the floor like a bag of dirty laundry. I quickly got my ass up out of there, walking back out the same way I walked in. She could have said whatever she wanted about me and my momma. Once she added my kids to the equation, I had no choice but to try to divide her ass in half.

————

I dropped my momma car back off and walked home. Just when I made it to my block now, I thought my eyes were deceiving me. My car was parked in front of my house, and

Uncle Junebug was sitting in one of the chairs on my front porch. He started heading toward my direction once he noticed me.

"I'm glad yo ass finally showed up. It's brick out here." I could tell he was cold. His nose was bright red. Uncle Junebug was out here looking like Rudolph with no Santa.

"What are you doing here? And how did my car get here? I'm so confused right now."

Uncle Junebug dangled my keys in front of me and smiled, taking some of the chill off his face.

"I got in touch with the tow company that dragged yo car away. Yo mother explained everythin' to me after you left the dinner. Her crazy ass remembered the name written on the truck." We both laughed.

My momma had the memory of an elephant; she didn't forget shit.

"Don't you ever sit over here in need and not tell me. Yo daddy was my best friend. I promised him on his deathbed I would take care of y'all. And I meant it."

Our dad passed away from lung cancer six years ago. That's another reason I hated that Denise smoked. I couldn't stand her ass, but I didn't want anything to happen to her either. She was still my sister. I could argue and fight with her but let someone else try that shit, and we would jump their ass.

"Thank you so much. I was too ashamed to come to you for help, and didn't want you to think of me as a failure or be disappointed."

Using the back of my hand, I wiped the tears from my eyes.

"I could never be disappointed in you or view you differently. You take care of those boys by yourself. The only time you have yo momma watch them is when you are workin' or handlin' business. I know because she told me." He hugged me with all his might, then held my face in his hands.

"Sorry, I'm an emotional mess right now."

"Don't apologize. You are my beautiful niece. An amazing mother, daughter, aunt, and sister. You continue to be yo authentic self and neva let your current circumstance negate everythin' you have done. I love you and always will, no matter what."

I cried so hard my ass looked like one of those damn memes. Uncle Junebug went in his pocket and pulled out a check made out to me for $5,000. I was completely at a loss for words. It felt like I was frozen in time.

"It ain't much, but it's enough to hold you over 'til you find another job. I also paid the balance that was left on your car, so that's one less bill you have to worry about. I'm gonna get on outta here. Y'all be good."

My uncle was a very special man. I couldn't believe he just did all of this for me and my boys. I would have him over for dinner next week. It was the least I could do after all he just did. Now, I could pay all my bills to zero and a few of them ahead.

I started thinking about my Valentine's Day date with Darius. If it was still with Mr. Herman, I would cancel that muthafucka with the quickness. But since his son took his place, it was about to go down!

# Chapter Six

ONE DAY BEFORE VALENTINES DAY

DELILAH

I couldn't get to the bank fast enough to deposit the check my uncle so generously gave me yesterday. We used the same bank, so the money was instantly available. The first thing I did, after paying my bills, was go to the store. I needed to get more stuff for my boys for Valentine's Day.

We always had breakfast together. During that time I gave them each a gift bag. I already had little bags made up of stuff I grabbed from the dollar store. It wasn't much because I was on a strict budget, but they weren't ungrateful children. They appreciate anything I gave them.

Now that I had a few extra dollars, I picked up stuff they needed. I got them each a pair of sneakers and two outfits. I couldn't wait to see their faces light up. They deserved this and so much more. My sons were growing up to be kind, respectable, young men, and that was because of me, their father, and Uncle Junebug.

My uncle stepped up because my boys had no male figures in their lives. He took them out twice a month, just to have one on one time with them. I was no longer with their father, Star, because once he was incarcerated, he decided it would be best if we just went our separate ways. Star didn't want me to have to put my life on hold because of the decisions he made.

He called our boys regularly and sent them weekly letters. Their father might not be able to be in their lives physically, but his presence was always felt. We were the best of friends, and I would put money on his account every week when I worked. I sent him a few dollars this week, now that my rent was caught up. Star always held us down when he was out, and I would always hold him down while he was incarcerated. He was serving a fifteen year sentence.

Our sons would be grown men by the time he got out. Hopefully, with all of us being consistent in their lives, my sons would remain on this path of greatness. And I hoped I could finally move on with my life, romantically. I never had another relationship after Star, therefore, I looked forward to my date with Darius on Valentine's Day. *I'm hoping it isn't our last.*

Speaking of my date, I had to figure out what I needed to get done for tomorrow. I could do my own hair, and I didn't wear makeup. I'd make sure my eyebrows were straight, do one of those ten minute facial masks, and throw on some lip gloss. Now, my hands and feet were a different story.

I was going to have to run out and get those professionally done. If I tried to do it myself, I would be up in here looking like one of my nieces did it. While I was out, I would see if I could find something to put on.

As I unlocked my car door to get in, something told me to look in the trunk. My purple bag was sitting right in there. Security must have tossed it back there for me when he walked me to my car. That night was crazy, and I must have been mad as hell to forget he did that. All this time I had no reason to even open the trunk. I tossed my bags in the front seat of my car.

Whatever the case, I have my bag now. I didn't need to buy something else to wear, and that saved me a trip to the mall. I would grab a small bottle of Dreft laundry detergent to wash my outfit in. It works great on anything, not just baby clothes. Plus, it was gentle and smelled good.

I would definitely have to let my outfit soak for a few hours before hand washing it to make sure there were no traces of that coyote smell on anything and let it air dry overnight. Everything started to fall in place, which let me know that the universe was working its magic for me.

# Chapter Seven

## DARIUS DANIELS

I was so smitten by the beauty of Delilah. The fact that she was extra fluffy was a turn on. I loved me a big woman. So did my father, which explained why he was so eager to go on this Valentine's Day date with Delilah. She probably reminded him of my mother when she was younger. They were similar in so many ways.

My parents divorced when I was in high school. My mom lived out on the West Coast with my sister. My father and I were very close. So, when she decided to relocate, I chose to stay with him. He was my best friend. I'm disappointed in his actions, though, and I informed him of my feelings after Delilah left.

Once he told me the entire background story of how he was even able to secure a date with Delilah, I was pissed. She gave me a brief run down, but he filled me in on all the missing pieces. I felt he took advantage of her situation. He used his power over her to basically force her into a compromising position.

Here was a mother who was down on her luck and instead of him taking pity on her, he used the situation to his advantage. She would do anything not to be put out. I'm quite sure Delilah didn't want to spend an evening with my pops. Shit, it was like being intimate with someone who could have been her dad.

Delilah probably felt it was her only way out of her predicament. I knew he didn't give her any other options. My father was only worried about feeding his own sexual appetite. There were services that could have helped her that he should have informed her about. The courts might have given her an extension once she explained her situation anyway. It wasn't easy to just evict people these days. They were lenient to renters.

I saw this side of my pops before. It was when my mother had decided to leave him for good. She had packed us up before in the past, leaving him alone, when we were younger. We would go to my auntie's house, then a week later be right back at home.

One day she finally had enough of his bullshit. I heard her tell him that he left her no choice. My mom felt like she had no other option, and said he basically forced her hand. I didn't know what she meant by that, and they never explained to us exactly why they divorced. I knew he visited the strip clubs often and felt that could have been one of the reasons.

I never questioned them about it, though. It wasn't my place as their child. Their personal business was just that, personal. If they didn't feel the need to tell us, who were we to ask? My parents' marriage had nothing to do with how they raised us. We weren't negatively affected by their decision not to stay together.

My sister would come to visit us here, and I would go visit them out there. Our parents made sure to never make their issues our issues. I did notice that after my mother left, he let himself go a little. I would keep up with the housework and cook for us, up until I left for the Air Force.

I would come home when I could, and he seemed to be just fine. My father managed to keep himself out of the rut he was once in. Now, the house looked like he fell back in it. Maybe being a landlord overwhelmed him, and that was why he asked me to take over. Whatever the reason, I'm here now and would make sure he was good.

Once I decided to take over the business, I did my research. I wanted to hit the ground running. My pops owned quite a few properties, and I wanted to make sure I was an efficient landlord. I would have ran into Delilah eventually. It was my plan to visit every home we owned.

I needed to introduce myself and make sure that everything was in working order. Who knew the last time my pops inspected their homes. From the way his house looked, he doesn't care about much these days. I'm definitely calling a cleaning service to get it in order. He lived like Mister from *The Color Purple*, before Celie came and after she left.

Delilah was definitely owed an apology, and I would give her one, on my father's behalf, when I saw her tomorrow. I felt like an excited kid the night before the first day of school. You wanted to go to sleep early because you couldn't wait for tomorrow to come, so you could wear your new outfit and sneakers. That was how I felt right now.

I really would like to get to know Delilah intimately. Life wasn't slowing down, and I damn sure wasn't getting any younger. I'm not interested in dating casually. I hoped to meet someone who knew what they wanted and was ready to settle down. Marriage was a goal of mine, and I wanted a family of my own.

Children would be nice, but it wasn't a deal breaker either. I just wanted someone to grow old with. Delilah mentioned she had children already, and she might not want anymore. Loving someone else's kids like my own wouldn't be a problem for me.

Family didn't always include biological members. I wasn't going to dream too far ahead, being that it was just one date. My hope was that it wouldn't be our last.

Looking down at my watch, it was time I stopped procrastinating and started preparing for tomorrow.

# *Chapter Eight*

## VALENTINE'S DAY - BREAKFAST

### DELILAH

Valentine's Day was finally here, and my boys were sitting at the kitchen table ready to throw down. I had the turkey bacon in the oven and was working on the heart shaped pancakes. I made the mix and poured it into a plastic bottle. My skillet was hot, and I coated it with a pad of butter. I made the outline of a heart with the batter, then filled it in.

We each got a stack of three pancakes, a few slices of bacon, and some fresh, squeezed orange juice. I literally squeezed the oranges myself with my manual juicer and garnished each glass with a sprig of fresh mint leaves and a few maraschino cherries.

While we were eating, everyone took turns saying what they

loved about our family. They knew it didn't have to be a long speech, like I always did. It just needed to be a few words on what warmed their heart.

I did it this way because it made them think about us as a family unit. It didn't matter how old they got, who they became in this life, or where they went in this world, we would always love and protect each other.

In my little speech I told them that they were the reasons I went so hard in life. They were my first thought when I woke up, and my last when I went to sleep. I let my sons know that they all gave me the same amount of joy in my heart, and I loved them like my last breath.

We finished up with breakfast, and they opened their bags while I got started on cleaning up the kitchen. I could hear the happiness in their "oohs" and "ahhs". They came running into the kitchen and enclosed me in a group hug. Of course they asked if they could wear one of the outfits and the sneakers.

I guess they wanted to look good going back over to their grandma's house. And that's right where I was getting ready to take them. I had to get ready for tonight. It had been so long since I entertained a man, and I started to get anxious.

Darius needed to have a great time. There was no doubt he was attracted to me physically; that was easy to see from his actions at the hospital. I wanted him to get to know me intimately as well. My goal was to connect with him on a higher level. After you got past the outer shell, what was on the inside of the person was what made you fall in love with them.

The way a person made you feel determined whether or not

you wanted to move forward. I need someone who could make me laugh. Someone who made me feel safe and secure when I was with him. A man that was willing to treat me like a queen because I damn sure would treat him like a king.

I also needed a man who knew how to take control of my body. He had to be able to handle all of this. I wanted him to enjoy the ride, but he also needed to be able to take me on one at the same time. Whew! Let me stop. I started getting excited just thinking about it. These kids should be ready by now.

"Boys, let's go! Momma got things to do. I'm 'bout to go start the car. Make sure y'all coats are zipped up and whoever is the last one out, close the door behind you."

I grabbed the two bags I put together for my nieces on my way out the door. They were always messing with my boys, but were still family. I got them something every holiday. It wasn't much, just a little something to let them know we thought of them. My nieces did appreciate it, and I had the boys sign the cards too.

We pulled up to my mom's house, and I beeped the horn, letting her know we were outside. I told my boys to go inside, and I would pick them up tomorrow afternoon. As they were getting out, my mom waved her hand at me to come on in too.

"Why do I have to come inside? I'm just dropping them back off. I'll talk to you later," I yelled after rolling down my window.

"Getcho nappy headed ass on up in here! Stop being so stubborn. Yo sister wants to see you." I reluctantly rolled my window back up, turned my car off, and got out.

"I just had my nails done and don't have time for any shenanigans. It's a day for love, not aggravation."

My mom hugged me and whispered in my ear to be nice as we entered the house. Denise was standing there with three gift bags in her hand when we walked inside. She gave one to each of my sons. I was a little taken back because usually she didn't get them anything. I never felt a way about it, and it had no effect on what I did for my nieces.

My mom sent all the kids into the room. Denise looked at me with sadness in her eyes. This was probably the first time I'd ever seen her actually look like she was remorseful. She grabbed onto both of my hands and took a deep breath.

"First off, let me apologize for my actions at dinner the other day. You had every right to react the way you did. Uncle Junebug tore into my ass after you left. Everything he said was correct. I just didn't want to hear it."

I couldn't believe my damn ears. She has never apologized to me, not once. I let her continue without interruption.

"After I stewed over everything he said, I came to the realization that I've always been a lil jealous of you. I was the popular one, but you were the confident one. You have always been so sure of yourself and lived in your truth every day. I had to act like someone else just to fit in. You didn't care about fitting in. They had to accept you as you were or get to stepping."

At this point, tears were sitting on my cheeks like fresh dew on the grass in the morning. I became very emotional. We had always been at odds with each other most of our lives and now, we could finally come to a truce.

Denise seemed so sincere in her words, so I was willing to forgive her. I hope she stood on everything she said and really wanted to be a better big sister to me.

"I'm blown away. I didn't even wanna come in, but I'm glad I did. Let's make a promise to each other that we will keep the past in the past. I accept your apology and just wanna be your sister, not your enemy."

We hugged each other; something we hadn't done since we were kids.

"Yes, agreed. We will make new memories from this day forward."

"Well, let me be on my way. I have a *real* date to get ready for."

I kissed my mom goodbye and yelled to the kids I would see them tomorrow.

# Chapter Nine

VALENTINE'S DAY – DINNER

DELILAH

**F**reek-A-Leek by Petey Pablo blasted through the speakers while I got myself together. It stayed on repeat because I needed music that was motivational. Every time I walked past the floor to ceiling mirrors that covered one of my living room walls, I stopped to pop my ass. A few twerks, then I was off again.

I had to stop playing around before time got away from me and finish cleaning the house from top to bottom. It was always together, but when someone came over I did a little extra. I picked up some new candles to burn too.

After placing two on the coffee table in the living room, I put one in the bathroom and two in my bedroom. I would light them fifteen minutes before he was set to arrive. My outfit was laid out on my bed. It dried completely, so I didn't have to use my hair dryer to help it along.

It was time for me to jump in the shower and hose myself down. I loved my detachable shower head. Being that I had extra folds and more to hold, I needed to be able to get up in all the crevices. My favorite body wash was rainbath by Neutrogena. It had such a fresh, clean scent and left you feeling and smelling amazing.

After my shower, I dried off and rubbed myself down with my homemade, shimmer body butter. It smelled of fresh citrus and vanilla. I added gold mica powder to it so when I put it on, it looked like my body was covered in glitter.

Darius wouldn't be able to resist me once he got a whiff of all this goodness. I put on my thong and bra. My fupa, fat upper pussy area, had turned into a hupa, huge upper pussy area. I was surprised those two pieces still fit, but I wasn't sure the boy shorts would.

They didn't have much give, and I would cry if I split the seam. I pulled them up and did the squat test. It was all good, so the only thing left to do was to cover it up. I planned on revealing my outfit during my striptease.

I put on the all white, split joint, v neck maxi dress I got online. It made me look angelic, but I planned on being devilish. Darius was in for the dance of his life tonight. Mr. Herman expected much more but since he was out of the picture, I wondered if that offer was still on the table.

Believe me, I wanted to serve myself up on a platter for

Darius. I just didn't want to chase him away. Maybe his dad didn't go into full details about the terms of our date. I couldn't worry about that right now. I needed to finish setting the ambiance. After placing Cayenne on my head, I went into the kitchen.

I was just going to put out some snacks because Darius texted me earlier not to worry about dinner. Mr. Herman gave him my number. He said he would grab it on his way here. I did pick up some beer, one light and one dark. A bottle of sweet red was chilling in the fridge alongside them.

When I finished lighting all the candles, my stomach did a little flip. I was starting to get nervous again. Once he arrived my nerves would calm down but right now, I started to freak out. It confused me because I was used to performing in front of people all the time, wearing next to nothing. Tonight, I was covered and acting like this was my first time entertaining a man. Taking in a deep breath, I told myself to calm down.

**Knock! Knock!**

I opened the door and Darius was standing there with flowers and a bag of groceries. He was full of surprises already.

"Hello, gorgeous! Happy Valentine's Day."

Darius greeted me as he placed the flowers in my hand and entered the house. I noticed he stepped right out of his sneakers before walking on the carpet.

He followed me to the kitchen, so he could put the bag down on the countertop. I took the black wool-blend hooded topcoat he wore and hung it up. Darius dressed casually in a pair of black fitted jeans and a charcoal gray sweater.

"Can you point me in the direction of the bathroom? I need to wash my hands." I showed him the way, then took my nosey ass back into the kitchen, so I could look in the bag.

"I hope you don't mind me taking over your kitchen for the night?"

When I turned around, Darius was standing there with a slight grin on his face.

"Not at all. I'm in total shock right now. I figured you would just buy dinner. I had no idea you planned on cooking. This is so sweet of you."

I smiled hard as hell like I just put Vaseline on my teeth.

"I'm glad you think so. I wanted to do something different. You were so generous to accept my invitation to replace my father, so it's the least I could do."

Lawd, this man was standing here talking to me, and all I could think about was my purple bag. I wanted to retrieve it and skip straight to dessert. The thoughts in my head were downright sinful. My hands were gripping the sides of my dress, making it move in a fanning motion. Feeling the heat between my thighs, I tried to cool myself down.

"Please tell me you aren't allergic to seafood because I want to make us some shrimp Alfredo. I did pick up chicken just in case you are."

Darius towered over me as he spoke.

"No, I'm not allergic, and that sounds delicious."

I started to get out the pots, pans, and utensils as he emptied the bag. Playing the role of his sous chef, I deveined, washed, and seasoned the shrimp while Darius started on the homemade Alfredo sauce.

He put three tablespoons of butter in a sauce pan and let it melt over medium low heat. To that, he added three tablespoons of flour. He stirred it until the flour mixed in with the butter, creating a roux.

Darius asked me to put on some water for the pasta. It wasn't boxed either, he had fresh pasta that you find in the refrigerated section. As I was doing that, he started to slowly pour a container of heavy cream into his pan. He didn't pour it all at once. Instead, he added in a little at a time, stirring the mixture constantly.

Once he was done pouring in the cream, he seasoned it with garlic powder, sea salt, and cracked black pepper. It started to smell amazing in here. I could see the sauce was starting to thicken up.

"I picked up a fresh wedge of Parmesan cheese and one already shredded, just in case you didn't have a cheese grater." He came prepared.

"You're in luck. I do have one."

I handed it to him, and he began to grate the cheese right into the pan. It started to melt instantly as it came in contact with the simmering sauce.

Darius added about a cup of cheese, put the fire on low, and continued to stir. By this time the water was boiling. I added some salt to the pot and grabbed the bottle of oil to put in there too, but he stopped me.

"Wait! What are you about to do." He laughed as he took the oil out of my hand.

"I always put a splash of oil in my water, so that the pasta doesn't stick as it's cooking. What's the issue?"

He put the oil down and added the pasta to the pot.

"You never put oil in your water. It will coat the pasta and prevent the sauce from being able to absorb into it."

Darius wasn't just charismatic but a damn chef too. I loved a man who could throw down in the kitchen as well as the bedroom. I prayed he could do both.

I had no plans on sleeping with this man. But if tonight went well and one day we happened to go there, I hoped he fucked like he cooked.

He continued stirring the sauce, and all I could think about was him bending me over the counter and fucking me like a porn star. I tried so hard to be a lady tonight and not a thot, but it wasn't working.

"Here, taste this and tell me what you think."

Darius took a spoon and scooped out a little bit of the sauce. He blew on it to cool it down before feeding it to me. It was like a scene out of a damn movie.

"Oh, wow, that's amazing! I'm never eating jarred Alfredo sauce again."

He mixed the pasta around with a pair of tongs. It didn't take long at all to cook. Instead of draining it, Darius took the pasta out of the water and put it directly into the sauce.

As he started on the shrimp, I got out the plates and wine

glasses. A dinner this elegant and fresh shouldn't be washed down with a bottle of beer.

I retrieved the wine from the fridge; it was nice and cold. After I pulled the cork out, I poured us up some and placed the glasses on the coffee table in the living room. We could relax on the couch as we enjoyed the feast he was preparing for us.

When I walked back into the kitchen, Darius chopped up some fresh broccoli and tossed it in the pan with the shrimp. It was the perfect pop of color the dish needed. I plated up the pasta, and he topped it off with the shrimp and broccoli. We took our food and grabbed a spot on the couch. It almost looked too good to eat. He really out did himself.

"I just want to say thank you right now before I start stuffing my face. It was so unexpected, and a girl could get used to this."

I stared right into his eyes. Darius needed to know how serious I was. No man has ever cooked for me.

Well, my dad did when we were growing up. He would whip up something here and there, but that doesn't count. I was talking about romantically. Usually I was the one in the kitchen slaving over the stove. Darius tried to spoil me already, and it was only our first date.

"You're very welcome. I'm honored to cook for such a beauty as yourself. Once you said we were staying in, I figured I would show off my culinary skills."

He licked his lips before digging into his food. I know longer had to worry about the damn crystals on my thong popping off. They would melt before the night was over if he kept this shit up. The way he licked his lips sent me into overdrive.

I pinched myself just to make sure I wasn't dreaming. Could the universe be kind enough to send this man into my life at the opportune time? Yes, it could because he was sitting right next to me.

"So, tell me about yourself, Delilah... I mean Dee. I want to know about the lovely woman who is still available to be pursued. Who let you slip from their grasp?"

Darius took a sip of his wine, sat his plate down, and shifted his body forward. He made sure he was fully focused on me to hear my response.

"Well, I'm a single mother of three handsome boys. They are my lifelines. I would truly be lost in this world without them. I'm currently unemployed, that's why I was behind on my rent in the first place. I've been trying to find work, but it's been hard."

"Oh, wow. I'm really sorry to hear that. Please continue."

I sat my plate down because my greedy ass had been talking and eating at the same damn time.

"Yeah, it's a lil tough, but I'll be okay. Their father is the one that released me from his grasp. He's incarcerated and didn't want me to be locked down as well. It was a selfless act on his part to want me to move on with my life. I would have done that bid with him if he hadn't forced me to walk away. I'm ten toes down when it comes to me and mine."

I took the last sip of my wine and got up to refill both of our glasses. When I stood to walk away, I heard Darius say "good lawd". It made me smile. My ass naturally sat up on my back, so I knew it was a sight for sore eyes in this dress.

Just for that, I made sure to bend over and put my ass in his face when I filled up our glasses. I switched hard as hell back into the kitchen to throw the bottle away. My crazy ass poured the rest of the wine right into our cups. We were both about to be tipsy. I also grabbed us each a beer.

"Why didn't any of those ladies in the Air Force, or in your travels, snatch you up? I know I would have. There would be eight kids running around here by now."

His eyes widened, then a smile appeared on his face.

"Damn, that's a lot of kids. Do you want a big family? Would you like to have more kids?"

"I would definitely have more kids for my husband. I want a lil girl; a mini me. I don't come from a big family, but I want one. I will fill this whole house up with kids for the right man."

He could tell I was serious as hell. It wasn't the wine talking. Darius cleared his throat before responding.

"That is music to my ears. I would love a large family as well. And to answer your question, I dated a few ladies during my time serving. It just didn't work out as I had hoped. I want someone I can share forever with. So, I decided to stop looking for love and let it find me."

He shrugged his shoulders and popped open his beer.

"What do you mean by letting it find you?"

At this point I gulped the wine. I was over sipping and trying to look cute.

"I figured the woman for me would appear out of nowhere when the time was right. There was no need to search for her because she was already being prepared for me. The universe would place her in my path when it saw fit." He took another sip of his beer, then grabbed my hand. "Hopefully you are that one... only time will tell."

Darius raised my hand up to his face and kissed it. All the juices in my body started flowing. He moved in closer and started leaving soft, wet kisses on my cheeks.

It had been so long since I felt the touch of a man. I thought I was about to cum at any moment, and all he did was kiss me. Darius rubbed on my exposed thigh and sucked on my neck and that was all she wrote. *I'm fucking him tonight.*

"Please let him respect me in the morning because I'm going for mine!"

I thought I was talking to myself inside my head, but I murmured it out loud.

"Oh, is that right?" he questioned with a smirk on his face.

Instead of answering him, I stood up and took a hold of his hand. We headed to my bedroom. I already had a plush chair sitting front and center for him. He took a seat while I started the music. I put together a playlist the other day. The only light we had was from the candles. They were the perfect ambiance.

*Can't Get Enough* by Tamia came on. I started lip singing to the song as I danced seductively for him. Now, I was in my element and in full control.

I swayed my hips from side to side as I slowly removed my dress, keeping up with the beat of the song. He took a deep breath and blew it out once he saw what I was wearing underneath. Someone else just made a guest appearance as well. And from the way it bulged through his pants, I could tell he got it from his daddy.

# *Chapter Ten*

DARIUS

When Dee took her dress off, my body started to react. I wasn't expecting her to be adorned in garments with such a beautiful array of colors. Her voluptuous body looked radiant, almost like it was glowing. My manhood felt the need to stand at attention.

He was all bent up in these jeans, waiting to be deployed. Dee came over to me, removed my sweater and tossed it on the floor. She was very seductive in her movements. The way her body swayed to the rhythm of each song had me in a trance.

Next, she removed the t-shirt I had on underneath, revealing my eight pack. She stood behind me, rubbing all over my chest and shoulders. I massaged her arms as she was touching me. Delilah placed gentle kisses on my shoulder blades. The touch of her soft lips sent a warm feeling throughout my body.

Now, she was in front of me and grabbed both of my hands, forcing me to stand up. She pulled down my jeans, finally releasing my soldier. He escaped from my boxer briefs and was ready for action. I stepped out of my jeans, kicked them to the side and removed the rest of my clothing.

Delilah pushed me back down onto the chair, turned around, and put her ass in my face. It took everything in me not to strip her down to nothing and slide right up in her. She rotated her ass in a circle, then made it bounce up and down.

I took hold of her hips, and she smacked my hands away. Delilah looked back at me and said, "You need to keep your hands to yourself, and I have a lil something to make sure you do."

She took a rope out of a purple bag she retrieved from under the bed and tied my hands behind my back. I wondered what else was in there. My father did mention he just wanted to experience why they called her *Jaws* one time, and said it had something to do with a purple bag.

I had no idea what he meant by that but hopefully, I was about to find out. Delilah sat on the edge of her bed, laid back, and had both feet in the air as she took her shorts off. She stood back up and when I saw she had on a thong, I wanted to bury my face right in the crack of her ass. All I could think about was sucking on those thick folds between her legs.

A faster pace song came on, and Delilah gave me a private

dance to be envied by all men. She was slipping and sliding all over her carpet. I watched in amazement as she did splits and dips while rubbing on her breast. Once her show was over, she untied me.

I was instructed to lay across the bed on my back. The next thing I knew, a warm cloth touched my skin. She wiped me down before putting a condom on my shaft. I watched as she poured some type of oil in her hand. A sweet smell filled the air that reminded you of the tropics.

The massage she applied to my legs was so relaxing and tantalizing at the same damn time. I wanted her in the worst way. The build up was enough to make me explode right now. Her hands move up and down my inner thighs like a skilled masseuse. Just when I thought the teasing was over, she had another trick up her sleeve.

Delilah pulled an ice cube from out of nowhere and started to rub it on the area behind my nut sack. She had a firm grip on my manhood at the same time, moving her hand up and down. Suddenly, I no longer felt the frozen block of water. It was replaced by her finger, which vigorously stroked the same sensitive area. I'd never experienced such an erotic sensation in all my life.

My toes curled up as I gripped the blanket. I was trying hard to fight the urge to release, but it was impossible. Once she started going faster, the stimulation caused me to bust. I came harder than water bursting through a cracked pipe.

I laid there, trying to collect myself while Delilah whipped out another warm rag to wipe me down again. No one has ever made me feel like this with their hands, or mouth for that matter.

"That was crazy! Now, it's my turn to please you."

I pulled her in close and kissed her juicy lips as I took off her bra. Delilah titties were bouncy and natural. I pushed them together, licking and sucking on her nipples as she moaned out loud.

Turning Delilah around, so I could remove her thong with my mouth, I reached into her purple bag to get the oil she used on me. I poured some in my hands and rubbed it all over her ass. I massaged each cheek separately, then together.

Her body relaxed while I rubbed more oil into her shoulders and back. I made sure to get under every roll, leaving no part untouched when I went back over her ass, then all the way down to her feet. I turned Delilah over and placed her in the middle of the bed.

Spreading her legs open, I slowly kissed the inside of her thighs. Even though I was ready to dive right in, I took my time. I showed love to every inch of her body, kissing and licking my way to her center, but I didn't indulge just yet.

I went back into her bag and found an insulated container with the ice cubes. She also has a container of mints in there. I popped two of them in my mouth, then I rubbed the ice cube all over her pussy lips. As I spread them apart, her jewel was exposed to the coldness, making her body react. She flinched, then moaned out with pleasure. It was now time to make Delilah scream my name!

# Chapter Eleven

DELILAH

Darius was in here about to make me lose my damn mind. *How is he using my own bag on me?* I saw him pop some of my sugar free Ice Breaker mints in his mouth. He was about to hit me with the cooling sensation that made you drip faster than a leaky faucet.

He looked me in my eyes, then took all of me in his mouth. A tingling sensation permeated every inch of my body while Darius continued to suck and lick on my pussy like he was trying to get to the center of my tootsie pop.

His tongue entered my cave. In and out it went, like he was diving for sunken treasures. He licked up and down the sides of my pearl before making it disappear into his mouth. Both of my legs convulsed uncontrollably as he pleased me to the point of eruption.

"Darius, oh my goodness. Darius!"

I couldn't help but scream out his name when my body released everything it had been holding in for years. His clean shaven face was covered in my juices. He got up and used his t-shirt to wipe off the remnants of my juices.

Reaching over, I grabbed a condom from the box I purchased yesterday. I was hoping to use them one day with him, if our lil date led to others, but I didn't think it would be tonight.

Darius stood in front of me while I sat on the edge of the bed. Taking the condom and putting it in my mouth, I placed it right in front of my teeth. I performed the motion of sucking his dick to get it to slide on and used my hand to make sure it was completely rolled out to the base of his dick, since he was so well endowed.

He pushed me back on the bed and spread my legs wide open. His hands rested on the back of my calves as he entered me. I watched as he slowly thrusted in and out. Darius pulled his dick it out just enough so that the tip stayed in, then made it disappear again.

Next thing I knew, he lifted me up and moved us into the middle of the bed. He never skipped a beat and dug in even deeper. His strokes were strong and fast. I wrapped my legs around him as he passionately kissed me. My moans were muffled by his lips while my body enjoyed every moment.

No words were spoken, but everything was understood. He pulled out and tapped me on my thigh. I turned around and positioned myself on the bed to where I was on my knees with my ass up and face down. He spread my legs further apart and slid right back in.

With his hands on my waist, Daruis started pounding away. I could feel the wetness dripping out of my pussy. It felt amazing and every time he collided with my ass, the wet slapping sound drove me insane.

He pulled out again and started licking up my juices from behind. I looked back and his face was buried in my ass. His hands pushed on the back of my thighs as he glided his tongue up and down the length of my pussy. I started throwing it back at him, fucking his face. Darius stiffened his tongue, so I tossed my ass faster and faster.

"Oh, yes! Right there, mmmmmm. Uhhhhh!" I moaned.

My clit swelled as the pleasure built up. I was almost at the point of orgasm.

"Don't cum! Get on top, so I can feel you as you do."

Darius laid down on the bed, resting his head on the pillows. I straddled him and lifted myself up a bit, so I could ease down on his thick dick, letting out a deep breath and a soft moan once I was flushed against him. I began to slowly rock back and forth, staring him right in his eyes.

I wanted to see his reaction as my tight pussy walls closed in on him. He gazed back at me while holding onto my hips. I placed my hands on his chest, leaned forward, and increased my speed. The whole bed was rocking at this point, and Darius moaned out in ecstasy; or he couldn't breathe. Either way, I wasn't stopping.

"Oh, Dee, you feel so good. Don't stop."

Darius whispered in my ear, and that was all the confirmation I needed to finish him off. I released him and repositioned myself, so that I was sitting over him like a frog on a lily pad. I took hold of his manhood and guided him back into my warmth.

I pressed my hands on his shoulders, close to his neck, as I bounced up and down. Darius got lost in the moment, reached up to run his hands through my hair, and pulled Cayenne off. He looked at me in a state of shock and confusion, still holding my wig in his right hand. I snatched Cayenne from his grasp and tossed her ass on the floor. It was my fault for not making sure she was pinned down.

Now, I was riding Darius with just a stocking cap on my head, which covered up my braids, looking like Rerun on *What's Happening* when he shaved his head bald and joined a cult. It didn't phase him one bit, though.

Darius smiled as he massaged the top of my head with both hands, then took one of my nipples into mouth. His tongue felt so good on my titties. He gave each of them some love. My knees were starting to ache, so I relaxed them into the straddling position.

We went back to rocking the bed like a boat. He wrapped his arms around me and squeezed tight, burying his face in my neck. I could feel his legs tighten underneath me. We both came simultaneously.

I rolled off of him and onto my back, feeling hot, sweaty, and a little out of breath. My pussy was throbbing, and my legs felt like a bowl of noodles. He was sprawled out next to me, staring up at the ceiling. I was finally able to collect myself enough to stand up and walk to the bathroom because I needed to pee and wash my ass.

If I was at his house, a bird bath would have been sufficient. But I was in my own shit and hopped in the shower real quick, so I could deep clean. I needed to be ready just in case there was a round two. Darius was still locked and loaded, even though he just emptied his clip.

It didn't take me long. I dried off and threw on my plush, pink robe. Darius probably had to use the bathroom too, so I decided to lotion up and stuff when I got back to my room. Remembering I was still wearing that damn stocking cap before I exited the bathroom, I peeled that muthafucka off and threw it in the trash.

As I walked down the hallway, I noticed Darius' coat was gone. I hurried to my room to see if he was there, but he wasn't. He disappeared like a ghost. And not Casper ass because he was friendly; more like Ghost from *Power*.

I couldn't believe he would do such a thing. He just left without saying goodbye, fuck you, nothing! It was like Darius was never here. So many emotions invaded my body all at once. I was hurt, sad, confused, and pissed all at the same time.

*What did I do to make him rush out of here like that?*

I thought we were having an incredible time. Maybe the whole wig snatching fiasco was too much for him. He did look in my purple bag; that could have scared him away. There were some things in there that weren't for everybody.

Did he change his mind about me because I gave it up after

only knowing him for two days? Darius wasn't a complete stranger. He was Mr. Herman's son. That had to count for something. I kept on racking my brain, trying to figure out the answers to all the questions popping up in my head.

I wanted to call him so bad, but I didn't want to look like some deranged woman or a stalker, even though his ass was in the wrong here. You don't do no tacky shit like that. I'd never felt so disrespected in my life. I thought there was something different about him, obviously I was wrong.

So many men tried to get with me, especially when I was dancing, but I never gave them the time of day. Darius came along, and I fucked him before we could even finish eating. I was drawn to him. Something about him allowed me to let my guard down. I knew we were moving fast, but I didn't think he would react like this. He really was on some sucka shit.

The fact that he was my landlord now made it even worse because I would feel awkward dealing with him in the future. I really couldn't believe he would do this to me. We needed to discuss what happened, but it won't be tonight. I decided to clean up, have another beer, then take my ass to bed.

# Chapter Twelve

DARIUS

I felt horrible running out on Dee like I just did. Especially after the amazing time we just shared. I wanted to stay and make love to her all night long but if I did, she probably would have freaked out. My dumb ass took one of my father's viagra pills on my way to her house.

Even though I wasn't a two pumps and a dump type of man, I wanted to be sure I would be able to keep up with her sexually if given the opportunity to enjoy her. Once Delilah started dancing, I knew she would throw that pussy on me for hours and was glad I had it in my system.

What I didn't know was how the little, blue pill was going to affect me. My father told me it increased your sexual performance and said I could take it even if I didn't have erectile dysfunction. But now I had an erection that wouldn't go away! I thought it would go limp after I busted my nut but no such luck. It stayed rock hard. When I heard Delilah start the shower, I figured it was the perfect time to leave without having to explain my situation.

Currently my dick still stood at attention, and if it didn't go down by morning, I would go to the emergency room. Hopefully, I didn't ruin my chances with Delilah. She was a special woman. There seemed to be a connection between us that was unexplainable. I felt it the moment I saw her at the hospital.

I'd never slept with a woman on our first date, and I damn sure didn't cook for them. Delilah and I were drawn together like two magnets. I knew she felt it as well and could tell when I was deep inside her.

Her body responded to me in a way no other woman had. Delilah was a free spirit who was so comfortable and confident with her body. Anybody else would have been horrified if I snatched their wig off, but she wasn't. She just kept right on going, giving me everything she had. That made me want her even more.

I kept checking my phone, expecting an angry text from her, cussing me out. I thought of calling Deliah, but I was such a coward because I reacted without taking her feelings into consideration. It made me feel like shit. Delilah probably thought it was something she did to chase me away. *What have I done?*

She would probably never speak to me again, unless it had

something to do with the house. And now I made that weird too. I needed to go to Delilah's house tomorrow and undo what I'd done. Meanwhile, I wrapped an ice pack in a towel, placed it on my dick, and hoped I could sleep my erection away.

# *Chapter Thirteen*

## DELILAH

I woke up early so I could have some time to myself. I ended up drinking a few more beers last night and felt the effects of it this morning. As I waited for the coffee I decided to make to finish brewing, Darius popped into my mind.

For the life of me, I still couldn't believe that muthafucka ran out like that. Last night was nothing short of amazing, and I was so comfortable with him. He devoured every inch of my body, making me feel like the most beautiful woman in the world.

**Knock! Knock!**

*Who the hell is knocking at my door this early in the morning?* I thought before I peeked out my window. It was Darius' monkey ass.

"What the fuck do you want?" I barked when I opened the door.

It was cracked just enough for him to see the hurt in my eyes.

"Dee, I am so sorry. If you let me in I can explain everything to you."

Darius stood on the porch, looking like someone just stole his dog. I was still very upset, but I allowed him to come in from the cold anyway.

"I can't wait to hear the lie yo ass 'bout to tell me."

"Dee, I would never lie to you! What I am about to tell you is the truth. The whole truth, whether you believe me or not."

He took off the hat and scarf he wore, placing them in his lap. Darius began to tell me everything that transpired after I left the room last night to jump in the shower. I couldn't help but laugh as he relieved his horrible situation. Darius was cracking up at himself too. I couldn't imagine how he felt, but that was no reason to abandon me the way he did.

"You could have told me, though. I would have understood and probably fucked on you until that muthafucka went limp, shit. It's every woman's dream to be locked in a room with a hard dick that will last for hours and hours."

"I am glad you are so understanding. I was nervous about coming here this morning."

He took off his coat now. I guess he planned on staying for a minute.

"Listen, you didn't judge me when I was looking like a hairless hedgehog when you snatched my wig off, so I won't hold this against you."

"And I promise it won't ever happen again. The wig snatching or me running out." We both fell out laughing.

Darius reached over, grabbing my face with both hands, and planted two juicy kisses on my lips. He laid me back on the couch and opened my robe. I was completely naked underneath. When I started rubbing on my pussy, his eyes almost popped out of his head.

After taking off all his clothes, Darius kneeled down before me. I lifted both of my legs up and rested them on his shoulders. He kissed on my plump lips before parting them with his fingers. His tongue collected all the sweetness that dripped out. My clit disappeared into his mouth, and he sucked on it until I quivered beneath him. This man sure knew how to please me.

"Run into my room and grab a condom outta my purple bag sittin' in the chair."

Before he got back, I was already on the carpet on all fours. I laid my robe down under me, so it could catch all the juices.

Hearing a buzzing sound, I looked up to see Darius wearing the vibrating dick ring that was in my purple bag, along with the condom. It was definitely much safer than him taking his father's viagra and would give him the satisfaction he was looking for.

Darius wasted no time entering me like he was sliding into home plate. We made love for what seemed like hours, taking breaks here and there to nestle in each other's arms.

"Who's cooking breakfast, me or you?" Darius questioned as we laid on the floor.

"I will since you cooked last night. Just help me up. It's easy for me to get down here, but you don't want to see how I get up." He laughed.

We headed to the bathroom and showered together. After we got out, he set the table while I started cooking and making my homemade strawberry lemonade. I could really get used to having a man around the house again.

I wouldn't introduce him to my boys until I knew for sure we were moving this, whatever it was, forward. They had only seen me with their father, so anyone else coming into their lives had to be committed to all of us. Darius would also have to understand my relationship with their father, and love my boys as if they were his own.

"The food is almost ready. I hope you are hungry because I think I made too much. I'm not used to cooking for two."

Darius came up behind me and kissed the nape of my neck, causing a soft moan to escape my lips.

"I'm going to eat everything you put in front of me, including you."

He spun me around, so that we were face to face.

"Thank you for spending Valentine's Day with your landlord. I know it's the next day, but we're picking up where we left off."

"You're welcome," I cooed.

I gave him an Eskimo kiss. My heart was full, and I could honestly say this was the happiest I had been in a long time.

# *Epilogue*

DELILAH

*TWO YEARS LATER...*

"Denise! Make them get down from that tree before they break their damn necks."

I swear my nieces did not listen because I already told them twice to stop climbing up there.

We threw a little family BBQ in our backyard. It was a beautiful day, so I told everyone they could come over and hang out. The hubby was on the grill, and I handled all the sides.

Darius and I got married last year at city hall. I didn't want a big ole wedding, so we had a small, intimate reception with our loved ones.

That day was also the end of my dancing career. Darius said he was the last man who would ever experience the contents of my purple bag. Those that had a taste of it at Big Worm's Rumpshakers better hold on to the memories.

I heard they had to close down after receiving so many code violations during a surprise inspection from the city. Keema and Kayla were now greeters at Walmart. The other clubs wouldn't hire them after finding out what they did to me. Big Worm ended up opening a car wash.

Darius hired me as his personal assistant once he found more deeds to properties his dad had purchased over the years that he wasn't aware of. The paperwork kept piling up, so he needed an extra set of hands to help sort everything out.

"Hey, Dee! What do you need me to help you do?" my momma questioned, being all loud as usual.

"Nothing! You always show up after everything is done."

They just got here, her and Mr. Cox. They ended up hooking up six months ago, and he was still hanging in there. The church finally lifted the ban they put on her ass, so she could play bingo again. My momma said when she went back, Mr. Cox was checking for her.

She let him chase after her for a minute, then finally gave in. His ass was turned on when my momma threatened to shock his balls. He said he liked feisty women, and she was the spark he needed. They be over at her house fucking like teenagers. Denise and her kids moved out, so she had the house to herself again.

My sister became a life coach after our healing. She finally found her calling and was killing it. They said experience was the best teacher. If that was the case, she had a Ph.D. in fucking up, so she damn sure could tell you what not to do. I was super proud of her, though, and she knew it.

"Mrs. Delilah Daniels, I'm going to need you to sit down and relax. I have a cheeseburger hot off the grill for you. Take a pause and feed my child."

Darius gave me the burger and a kiss on the cheek. He became so overprotective ever since we found out I was pregnant.

We were expecting our first child together, a little girl, who would be here in the next few months. I couldn't believe I started all over again, but I was excited to meet her. She had three big brothers that were ready to spoil and love on her forever.

My sons absolutely adored Darius. He did everything, including going out twice a month with them and Uncle Junebug. It was a family affair, and I loved it.

They still keep in regular contact with their dad. Star will always be their father, no one could replace him. My boys just had an extra person to love them and make memories with. They called him Double D, and I called him Big D.

After I finished putting the drinks on ice I took a seat on the deck, in between my momma and Denise. I watched everybody laughing and having a great time. It made me a little teary eyed because I was going to miss this house. There wasn't enough room here for our growing family, so we had Darius' family house renovated.

Mr. Herman ended up moving to the West Coast with his ex-wife and daughter. They flew out here to visit him while he was in rehab, and realized he was suffering from depression. His daughter felt it was best if he went back with them, and her mother agreed. Neither one of them had moved on since the divorce. They were able to rekindle their love for each over these last two years.

"Whew, them boys tired me out. I need a cold drink."

Uncle Junebug could barely breathe as he took a seat on the steps. He had walked the boys to the park around the corner to play basketball.

"I just put some beers on ice too. Grab you one from the cooler and kick back."

At the end of the day, there was nothing better than giving and receiving love!

**HAPPY VALENTINE'S DAY!**

# Author Charisse C Carr's Catalog

A Countdown To His Love

https://amzn.to/3CbVXJL

Harper & Stone: A Family Affair

https://bit.ly/442pD8f

Mali & Chaquille: A Dangerous Hood Love

https://amzn.to/3hQUf9i

Mali & Chaquille: A Dangerous Hood Love 2

https://amzn.to/3DlGBTD

The Asaad Brothers

https://a.co/d/7UxFfq8

The Asaad Brother: A Hitta's Revenge

https://a.co/d/2ufRR7O

Anthologies

Toxic Traits: A Collection of Domestic Violence Short Stories

https://a.co/d/f9CgFQh

# Social Media:

Click on the link below to follow me on Facebook!

https://www.facebook.com/profile.php?id=100077944875169&mibextid=eHce3h

Click on the link below to follow me on Instagram!

https://www.instagram.com/authorcharisseccarr?igsh=Z3FtcWtwdjl6ZWt6&utm_source=qr

Click on the link below to follow me on TikTok!

https://www.tiktok.com/@authorcharisseccarr?_t=8ibAddJaArz&_r=1

Made in the USA
Columbia, SC
05 May 2025

57559572R00061